Having got this
how to procee
prowled around
thrust into his pockets and his brows drawn together.

"I've been thinking about what you said," he said at last, coming to a halt by the window.

"What *I* said? When?"

He turned to look at her.

Telltale color crept into Lou's cheeks. Trust Patrick to bring that up now, just when she had allowed herself to relax and think that the whole sorry incident was forgotten.

"I shouldn't pay any attention to anything I said that night." She tried to make a joke of it. "I'd had far too much champagne."

"You said I should think about marrying you," said Patrick. "And that's what I've been doing. I think you were right. I think we should get married."

Jessica Hart had a haphazard career before she began writing to finance a degree in history. Her experience ranged from waitress, theater production assistant and Outback cook to newsdesk secretary, expedition PA and English teacher, and she has worked in countries as different as France and Indonesia, Australia and Cameroon. She now lives in the north of England, where her hobbies are limited to eating and drinking, and traveling when she can, preferably to places where she'll find good food or desert or tropical rain. If you'd like to find out more about Jessica Hart, you can visit her Web site at www.jessicahart.co.uk

Books by Jessica Hart

HARLEQUIN ROMANCE®

3797—HER BOSS'S BABY PLAN
3820—CHRISTMAS EVE MARRIAGE

CONTRACTED: CORPORATE WIFE

Jessica Hart

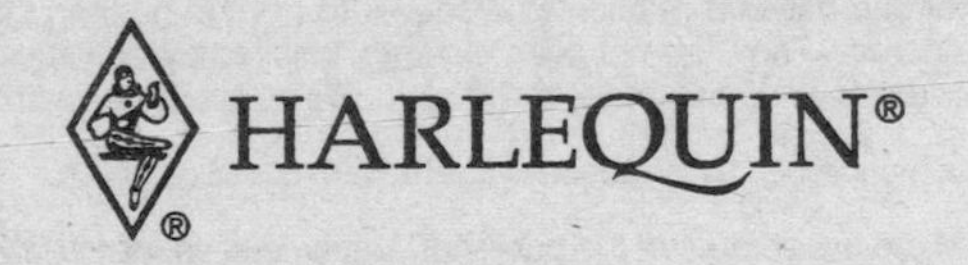

TORONTO • NEW YORK • LONDON
AMSTERDAM • PARIS • SYDNEY • HAMBURG
STOCKHOLM • ATHENS • TOKYO • MILAN • MADRID
PRAGUE • WARSAW • BUDAPEST • AUCKLAND

For Diana, with love

ISBN 0-373-03861-5

CONTRACTED: CORPORATE WIFE

First North American Publication 2005.

This edition published by arrangement with Harlequin Books S.A.

www.eHarlequin.com

Printed in U.S.A.

CHAPTER ONE

THE lift doors slid open, and out stepped Louisa Dennison, bang on time. As always.

Watching her from across the lobby, Patrick was conscious of a familiar spurt of something close to irritation. Dammit, couldn't the woman be five seconds late for once?

Here she came, in her prim little grey suit, whose skirt stopped precisely at the knee, not a hair of her dark head out of place. She looked sensible, discreet, well groomed, the epitome of a perfect PA.

Patrick knew that he was being irrational. He had been lucky to inherit such an efficient assistant when he'd taken over Schola Systems. Lou—her name was the only relaxed thing about her, as far as he was concerned—was a model secretary. She was poised, punctual, professional. He never caught her gossiping or making personal phone calls in the office. She showed no interest whatsoever in his personal life, so Patrick never felt obliged to ask about hers. No, he couldn't ask for a better PA.

It was just that sometimes he found himself wishing that she would make a mistake, just a little one. A typing error, say, that he could pick her up on, or a file that she couldn't lay her hand on immediately. Maybe she could ladder her tights, or spill her coffee. Do something to prove that she was human.

But she never did.

The truth was that Patrick found Lou secretly intimidating at times, and it annoyed him. If there was any intimidating to be done, he was the one who liked to do it. Grown men had been known to tremble when he walked into the room, and his reputation as a ruthless executive was usually enough to make people tread warily around him.

Not Lou Dennison, though. She just looked at him with those dark eyes of hers. Her expression was usually one of complete indifference, but sometimes he suspected it also held a quiet irony that riled Patrick more than he cared to admit. It wasn't even as if there was anything particularly special about her, he thought with a tinge of resentment. She was attractive enough, but she had to be at least forty-five, and it showed in the lines around her eyes.

That cool, composed look had never done anything for him, anyway. He liked his women more feminine, more appealing, less in control. And younger.

'I'm not late, am I?' Lou asked as she came up to him, and Patrick repressed the urge to glance ostentatiously at his watch and announce that she was a good fifteen seconds overdue.

'Of course not.'

He forced a smile and reminded himself that it wasn't actually Lou's fault that high winds had forced the closure of the east coast line that evening, that it was too far to an airport, or that he would rather be having dinner with almost anyone else. There had been no way he could have got out of asking her to share a meal with him since they were both stranded, but he was hoping they could get it over with quickly and then go their separate ways for the rest of the evening.

He nodded in the direction of the restaurant. 'Shall we go straight in? Or would you like a drink first?'

The drink option was such a patent afterthought that Lou was left in little doubt that Patrick was looking forward to their meal with as little pleasure as she was. Clearly she was supposed to meekly agree to eating straight away, but Lou didn't feel like it.

She'd had a long day. It had begun with a five o'clock alarm call, progressed to getting two squabbling adolescents out of the house earlier than usual, continued with delays on the tube, followed by a stressful train journey with Patrick Farr. This was the first time they had had to travel to secure a contract, and she hadn't thought her presence was necessary, but Patrick had insisted.

In the end, the meeting had been successful, but it had been long and intense, and Lou had been looking forward to getting home and enjoying a rare evening on her own to wind down with a stiff gin and a long bath without her children banging on the door and demanding to know what there was to eat or where she had put their special pair of torn jeans, which they needed right *now*.

And now she was stuck in this hotel with her boss instead. It wouldn't have been too bad if Patrick hadn't felt obliged to invite her to have dinner with him, or if she'd been able to think of a way of refusing without sounding ungracious. As it was, it looked as if they were both condemned to an evening of stilted conversation, and for that she definitely needed a drink!

'A drink would be lovely, thank you,' she said defiantly, ignoring the way Patrick's thick brows drew together. He was evidently a man who was used to getting what he wanted—especially as far as women were concerned, if rumours were anything to go by. No doubt Lou was expected to fall in with his wishes like everyone else.

Tough, she thought unsympathetically. If he didn't like it, he shouldn't have asked her!

'Let's try the bar, then,' he said, with just the suggestion of gritted teeth.

Lou didn't care. In the three months since Patrick Farr

had taken over Schola Systems he had made it obvious that he had no interest whatsoever in his new PA. Not young and pretty enough, clearly, Lou thought dispassionately. She didn't mind that, but she didn't see why she should pander to his ego in her free time. She wasn't actually working this evening, and it wouldn't do Patrick Farr any harm not to get his own way for once.

The bar was even worse than Patrick had feared. By the time they had realised that there would be no more trains to London that night, and that all road and air traffic was equally disrupted by the weather, all the best hotels had been booked out.

It was a long time since he had stayed anywhere this provincial, he thought, looking around the bar with distaste. It was overflowing with vegetation, and so dark that they practically had to grope their way to a table, which did nothing to improve his temper.

'What would you like?' he asked Lou as he snapped his fingers to summon the barman, although whether the man would be able to find them in the gloom was another matter.

'A glass of champagne would be nice,' said Lou composedly as she settled herself and smoothed down her skirt.

Patrick was surprised. She hadn't struck him as a champagne drinker. He would have thought champagne too fizzy and frivolous for someone so efficient. He could imagine her drinking something much more sensible, like a glass of water, or possibly something sharp. A dry martini perhaps. Yes, he could see her with one of those.

Lou lifted her elegant brows at his expression. 'Is that too extravagant?' she asked, thinking that a glass of champagne was the least that he owed her after the day she had had. And it wasn't as if he couldn't afford it. The Patrick

Farrs of this world could buy champagne by the truckload and think of it as small change.

'We did win that contract,' she reminded him, a subtle edge to her voice. 'I thought we should celebrate.'

'Of course.' Patrick set his teeth, perfectly aware that he should have suggested a celebration given the size of the contract they had just won. 'I'll have the same.'

The barman had fought his way through the artificial jungle and was hovering. Opening his mouth to ask for two glasses of champagne, Patrick changed his mind and ordered a bottle instead. He wasn't going to have Lou Dennison thinking that he was mean.

'Certainly, sir.'

Sitting relaxed in her chair, she was looking around the gloomy bar, apparently unperturbed by the silence while they waited for the barman to come back. She was quite unlike the women he was usually with in bars, Patrick reflected. He liked girls who were prepared to enjoy themselves a bit.

Take Ariel, for instance. Ariel was always *thrilled* to be out with him. That was what she told him, anyway. If she were here, she'd be chatting away, entertaining him, exerting herself to captivate him.

Unlike Lou, who was just sitting there with that faintly ironic gleam in her eyes, unimpressed by his company. What would it take to impress a woman like her? Patrick wondered. Someone must have done it once. She was Mrs Dennison, although he noticed that she didn't wear a wedding ring. Divorced, no doubt. Her husband probably couldn't live up to her exacting standards.

Uncomfortable with the situation, Patrick leant forward and picked up a drinks mat, tapping it moodily on the low table between them. It took a huge effort not to glance at his watch, but chances were he wouldn't be able to read it anyway in this light. It looked like being a long evening.

Lou was thinking the same thing. Patrick's moody tapping was driving her mad. It was just the kind of thing Tom did when he was being at his most annoying. Her fingers twitched with the longing to snatch the mat out of his hand and tell him to stop fiddling at *once*, the way she would if Tom were sitting there irritating her like this.

But Tom was her son and eleven, while Patrick Farr had to be in his late forties and, more to the point, was her boss. And she couldn't afford to lose her job. She had better hold back on the ticking-off front, Lou decided reluctantly.

She was gasping for a drink. Where was that champagne? The barman must be treading the grapes out there. It couldn't take that long to shove a bottle in an ice bucket and find a couple of glasses, could it? If it didn't arrive soon, she was going to have to take that mat anyway and shove it—

Ah, at last!

Lou smiled up at the barman as he materialised out of the gloom, and Patrick's hand froze in mid-tap as he felt a jolt of surprise. He hadn't realised that she could smile like that.

She never smiled at *him* like that.

She smiled, of course, but it was only ever a cool, polite smile, the kind of smile that went with her immaculate suit, her perfectly groomed hair and her infallible professional manner. Not the warm, friendly smile she was giving the barman now, lighting her face and making her seem all at once attractive and approachable. The kind of woman you might actually want to share a bottle of champagne with, in fact.

Patrick sat up straighter and studied her with new interest

as the barman opened the bottle with an unnecessary flourish and made a big deal of pouring the champagne.

The boy was clearly trying to impress Lou, Patrick thought disapprovingly, watching his attempts at banter. She had only smiled at him, for heaven's sake. Anyone would think that she was hot, instead of nearly old enough to be his mother. Just what they needed, a barman with a Mrs Robinson fixation.

And now he was tossing his cloth over his shoulder in a ridiculously affected way as he placed the bottle back in the ice bucket, and telling Lou to enjoy her drink. Patrick noticed that *he* didn't get so much as a nod, which was a bit much given that he was paying for it all.

'Thank you,' Lou was saying, with another quite unnecessary smile.

Patrick glowered at the barman's departing back. 'Thank God he's gone. I was afraid that he was planning on spending the whole evening with us. I'm surprised he didn't bring himself a glass and pull up a chair.'

'I thought he was charming,' said Lou, picking up her glass.

She would.

'Don't tell me you've got a taste for toy boys!'

'No—not that it would be any business of yours if I did.'

Patrick was taken aback by her directness. She was normally so discreet.

'You don't think it would be a bit inappropriate?' he countered.

Lou stared at him for a moment, then sipped at her champagne. 'That sounds to me like a prime case of pots and kettles,' she said coolly, putting her glass back down on the table.

'What do you mean?' demanded Patrick.

'I understand that your own girlfriends tend to be on the young side.'

Patrick was momentarily taken aback. 'How do you know that?'

She shrugged. 'Your picture is in the gossip pages occasionally. You've usually got a blonde on your arm, and I've got to say that most of them look a good twenty years younger than you.'

That was true enough. Patrick didn't see why he should apologise for it. 'I like beautiful women, and I especially like beautiful women who aren't old enough to get obsessed with commitment,' he said.

Ah, commitment-phobic. That figured, thought Lou with a touch of cynicism. She knew the type. And how. Lawrie had never been hot on commitment either, but at least he had warmth and charm. Patrick didn't even have that to recommend him.

She studied him over the rim of her glass. He was an attractive enough man, she admitted fairly to herself. Mid to late forties, she'd say. Tall, broad-shouldered, well set up. He had good, strong features too, with darkish brown hair and piercing light eyes—grey or green, Lou hadn't quite worked that one out yet—but there was a coolness and an arrogance to him that left her quite cold. He seemed to go down well with young nubile blondes, but he certainly didn't ring any of *her* bells.

Not that that was likely to bother Patrick Farr much. She was a middle-aged woman and it was well known that you became invisible after forty, particularly to men like him. She doubted that he had registered anything about her other than her efficiency.

'I'd no idea you took such an interest in my personal life,' Patrick was saying, annoyed for some reason by her dispassionate tone.

'I don't. It's absolutely nothing to do with me.'

'You seem to know enough about it!'

'Hardly,' said Lou. 'The girls in Finance have taken to passing round any articles about you so that we can get some idea of who's running the company now. You took us over three months ago, and all we know about you is your reputation.'

'And what is my reputation, exactly?' asked Patrick.

Lou smiled faintly. 'Don't you know?'

'I'd be interested to hear it from your point of view.'

'Well...' Lou took a sip of her champagne—it was slipping down very nicely, thank you—and considered. 'I suppose we'd heard that you were pretty ruthless. Very successful. A workaholic, but a bit of a playboy on the side.' Her mouth turned down as she tried to remember anything else. 'That's it, really.' She glanced at him. 'Is it fair?'

'I like the successful bit,' said Patrick. 'As for the rest of it...well, I certainly work hard. I know what I want, and I always get what I want. I like winning. I'm not interested in compromising or accepting second best. If people think that's ruthless, that's their problem,' he said. Ruthlessly, in fact.

'And the playboy side?'

He made a dismissive gesture with his glass. 'People only say that if you're rich and don't tie yourself down with a wife and children. I like the company of beautiful women, sure, and I meet lots of them at the parties and events I'm invited to, but I'd much rather work than swan around on yachts or waste money in casinos or whatever it is playboys do.'

'I see. I'll tell the girls in Finance that you're really quite boring after all, then.'

Patrick looked up sharply from his glass and met Lou's

eyes. They held a distinct gleam of amusement and he realised to his amazement that she was teasing him.

There was a new sassiness to her tonight, he thought, and he wasn't at all sure how to take her. Lou Dennison had always been the epitome of an efficient PA, quiet, discreet, always demurely dressed in a neat suit, but he had had no sense of her as a woman beyond that.

Now, suddenly, it was as if he were seeing her for the first time. The dark eyes held a challenging spark, and there was a vibrancy and a directness to her that he had never noticed before. Patrick's interest was piqued. Perhaps there was more to Lou than was obvious at first glance.

He knew nothing about her, he realised. If he'd thought about it at all, he might have imagined her going home to an immaculately organised flat somewhere, but the truth was that he had never really considered the fact that she had any existence at all outside the office. What did she do? Where did she go? What was she really like?

He ought to know, Patrick thought with a twinge of shame. She had been his PA for three months. Of course, they had been incredibly busy trying to turn the failing firm around, and she wasn't exactly easy to get to know. She never encouraged any form of social contact...or was it just that he had been too intimidated by her composure to make the first move?

Patrick wriggled his shoulders uncomfortably. He should have made more of an effort. She was the closest member of staff to him, after all. The truth was that he was more used to women flirting and fluttering around him. No way would Lou Dennison indulge him like that. She wasn't the flirting kind.

On the other hand, what did he know? Maybe it was time to find out more about her.

'So what about you?' he asked her. 'Do you live up to *your* reputation?'

Lou looked surprised. Well, that was better than indifference or irony, anyway.

'I don't have a reputation,' she said.

'Yes, you do,' Patrick corrected her. 'I heard all about you before I got to Schola Systems. I heard that it was you that ran that company, not Bill Sheeran.'

Lou frowned. 'That's rubbish!'

'Don't worry, I don't believe it for a minute. If you'd been running the company, you would never have let it go under. You're too competent to let that happen.'

She grimaced slightly. 'Competent?' It didn't sound very exciting. Not like being a playboy. 'Is that what people think of me?'

Her glass was empty. Patrick lifted the bottle and held it over the ice bucket to let it drip for a moment. 'Competent...efficient...practical...yes, all those things.'

'You don't have much choice about being practical when you've got kids to bring up on your own,' said Lou with a sigh.

'It's easy to be laid-back when you've just got yourself to worry about,' she said, oblivious to the fact that his head had jerked up in surprise. 'It's different when the rent is due and there are bills to be paid and every morning you've got a major logistical operation just to get the kids up and dressed and fed, and to check that they've got everything they need and that all their homework is done and that they're not going to be late for school.'

Patrick hadn't got over the first revelation. 'You've got *kids*?' he said, ignoring the last part of her speech. He stared at her. Children meant mess and chaos and constant requests for time off, none of which he associated with Lou Dennison.

She had raised her brows at the incredulity in his expression. 'Just two. Grace is fourteen, and Tom's eleven.'

'You never mentioned that you had children,' said Patrick accusingly.

'You never asked,' said Lou, 'and, to be honest, I didn't think you'd be the slightest bit interested in my private life.'

He hadn't been—he *wasn't*, Patrick reminded himself—but, still, she might have said something. He felt vaguely aggrieved. Two children, adolescent children at that, were a big thing not to mention.

'Why have you kept them a secret?'

'I haven't,' said Lou, taken aback. 'There's a framed photo of both of them on my desk. If you're that interested, I'll show you tomorrow!'

'There's no need for that, I believe you,' said Patrick, recoiling. He had no intention of admiring pictures of grubby brats. 'I was just surprised. I've had secretaries with children before, and they were always having time off for various crises,' he complained. 'After the last time, I vowed I'd never have a PA who was a mother again.'

'Very family-minded of you,' said Lou.

Patrick's brows drew together at the unconcealed sarcasm in her voice. 'I haven't got anything against families,' he said. 'It's up to individuals whether they have a family or not, but I don't see why I should have to rearrange my life around other people's children. I had a PA once whose children ended up running the office. We'd just be at a critical point of negotiations, and Carol would be putting on her coat and saying that she had to get to the school.'

'Sometimes you just have to go,' said Lou, who had somehow managed to get to the bottom of another glass of champagne. 'Especially when your children are smaller. At least my two are old enough to take themselves to and from school, but if anything happened, or they were ill, then I'm afraid that I would be putting on my coat too.'

Patrick looked at her as if a dog he had been cajoling had just turned and snapped at him, but he refilled her glass anyway. 'Am I supposed to find that reassuring?'

'I'm just telling you, that's all,' said Lou. She looked at him directly. 'Is it going to be a problem for you that I have children?'

'Not as long as they don't interfere with your work,' said Patrick.

'You know that they don't, or you would have known about their existence long before now,' she said in a crisp voice. 'That doesn't mean there won't be times when I *will* need to be flexible, and, yes, sometimes at short notice.'

'Oh, great.' Patrick hunched a shoulder and Lou leant forward.

'You're obviously not aware of the fact that Schola Systems has always had a very good reputation for family-friendly policies,' she admonished him. 'I was lucky to get a job there when I had to go back to work and the children were small, and especially to have such an understanding boss. Bill Sheeran was always flexible when people needed time at home for one reason or another.

'It won him a lot of loyalty from the staff,' she added warningly, 'so if you were thinking of holding parenthood against your employees, you might find yourself without any staff at all!'

'There's no question of holding anything against anyone,' said Patrick irritably.

He didn't want to hear any more about how marvellous Bill Sheeran had been. Not marvellous enough to save his own company, though, Patrick thought cynically. It was all very well being friendly and flexible, but if Patrick hadn't taken over all those admiring employees would have been spending a lot more time at home than they wanted. There was no point in being family friendly if your firm went bust and your staff found themselves out of a job.

'I just wish you'd told me, that's all,' he grumbled to Lou.

Lou didn't feel like making it easy for him. Honestly, the man never even asked her if she'd had a nice weekend on a Monday morning. 'If you'd shown any interest in your new PA at all, you would have known.'

'I'm showing an interest now,' he said grumpily. 'Is there anything else I need to know?'

'Is there anything else you want to know?' she countered.

'You don't wear a wedding ring,' said Patrick after a moment.

'I'm divorced. Why?' The champagne was definitely having an effect. 'Don't tell me you've got a problem with divorce as well as children?'

'Of course not. I'm divorced myself.'

'Really?'

'Why the surprise? It's not exactly uncommon as you'll know better than anyone.'

Quite, thought Lou. 'You're right. I don't know why I was surprised, really. I suppose it's because you don't seem like the marrying kind,' she said, thinking of his lifestyle. Playboy or not, he clearly didn't spend much time at home.

'I'm not,' said Patrick with a grim smile. 'That's why I'm divorced. We were only married a couple of years. We were both very young.' He shrugged. 'It was a mistake for both of us. That'll be a bit of news for the girls in Finance,' he added, not without a trace of sarcasm.

'I'll pass it on,' said Lou, smiling blandly in return.

Patrick held up the bottle and squinted at the dregs in surprise. 'We seem to have finished the bottle,' he said, sharing out the last drops and upending it in the ice bucket. 'Do you want another? Your toy boy is probably longing for an excuse to come over and see you again!'

Lou rolled her eyes. 'I think I'd better eat,' she said, ignoring the toy-boy crack.

The champagne had slipped down very nicely. A little too nicely, in fact. She was beginning to feel pleasantly fuzzy. She might even be a bit tipsy, Lou realised, hoping that she would be able to make it to the restaurant without falling over or doing anything embarrassing. They hadn't had time for a proper lunch and it was all starting to catch up with her.

She felt better in the restaurant. The waiters fussed around, bringing bread and a jug of water without being asked. Obviously they could see that she needed it.

Lou took a piece of bread, and spread butter on it. This was no time to worry about her diet. She needed to line her stomach as quickly as possible.

She tried to focus on the menu, but kept getting distracted by Patrick opposite. He had been easier to talk to than she had expected. Of course, the champagne had probably helped. He certainly wasn't as brusque and impersonal as usual. She had even found herself warming to him in a funny kind of way. It was as if they had both let down their guards for the evening. It must be something to do with being stranded away from home and tired...and, oh, yes, the champagne.

She really mustn't have any more to drink, Lou decided, but somehow a glass of wine appeared in front of her and it seemed rude to ignore it. She would just take the occasional sip.

'So,' said Patrick when they had ordered. 'What's happened to your children tonight? Are they with their father?'

'No, Lawrie lives in Manchester.' There was a certain

restraint in her voice when she mentioned her ex-husband, he noticed. 'I knew I'd be late back to London even if the trains had been running, so I arranged for them to stay with a friend. They love going to Marisa's. She lets them watch television all night and doesn't make them eat vegetables.'

Which was probably more than Patrick needed or wanted to know. He was only making polite conversation after all. She was getting garrulous, a sure sign that she had had too much to drink. Better have another piece of bread.

'Have you got any children?' she asked, thinking it might be better to switch the conversation back to Patrick before she started telling him how good at sport Grace was or how adorable Tom had been as a baby.

'No,' said Patrick, barely restraining a shudder at the very idea. 'I've never wanted them. My ex-wife, Catriona, did. That's one of the reasons we split up in the end.' His mouth pulled down at the corners as he contemplated his glass. 'Apparently I was incredibly selfish for wanting to live my own life.'

Lou frowned a little owlishly. 'But isn't the reason you get married precisely because you want to live your life with another person, that you want to do it together and not on your own?'

She'd spoken without thinking and for a moment she thought she might have gone a bit far.

'I told Catriona before we got married that I didn't want children,' said Patrick, apparently not taking exception at the intrusiveness of her question. 'And she said that she understood. She said she didn't want a family either, that she didn't want to share me with anyone else, not even a baby.'

He rolled his eyes a little as if inviting her to mock his younger self who had believed his wife, but Lou thought she could still hear the hurt in his voice. He must have loved Catriona a lot.

'We *agreed*,' Patrick insisted, even as part of him marvelled that he was telling Lou all this. 'It wasn't just me. I thought we both wanted the same thing and that everything would be fine, but we'd hardly been married a year before she started to lobby for a baby.'

He sounded exasperated, and Lou couldn't help feeling a pang of sympathy for poor Catriona. You'd have to be pretty brave to lobby Patrick Farr about anything.

'It's quite common for women to change their minds about having a baby,' she said mildly. 'It's a hormone thing. You can be quite sure you're not interested, and then one day you wake up and your body clock has kicked in, and suddenly a baby is all you can think about. I was like that before I had Grace.'

'Yes, well, I've learnt the hard way that women change their minds the whole time,' said Patrick grouchily. 'If I'd known then what I know now, I wouldn't have believed Catriona in the first place. But I was young then, and it was a blow.'

'It must have been a blow for her too,' Lou pointed out. 'It doesn't sound as if you were prepared to compromise at all.'

'How can you compromise about a baby?' demanded Patrick. 'Either you have one or you don't. There are no halfway measures, no part-time options, on parenthood.'

That would be news to Lawrie, Lou couldn't help thinking. He seemed to think that he could drop in and out of his children's lives whenever it suited him.

'Plenty of fathers don't have much choice but to see their children on a part-time basis,' she said, struggling to sound fair. 'It can work.'

'I didn't want to be a father like that,' said Patrick flatly. 'I don't believe in half measures. Either you do something properly, or you don't do it at all.'

Not the king of compromise, then.

CHAPTER TWO

'YOU could say that about marriage too,' said Lou, courage bolstered by all the champagne she had drunk.

Patrick twisted a fork between his fingers, his expression bitter. 'I would have stuck with our marriage no matter what, but Catriona wanted a divorce. So that's what happened. We didn't do it at all.'

'What happened to Catriona?'

'Oh, she met someone else. She got her children...three of them...but now she's divorced again. Her husband ran off with his secretary for a more exciting and child-free life, I gather, so she's on her own again.'

'You know,' he confided slowly, 'Catriona always used to say that if only she could have a baby, she would never be unhappy again, but I still see her occasionally, and she doesn't look very happy to me. She's got the children she wanted, but she looks exhausted and worn down.'

'I'm not surprised if her husband's left her and she's dealing with three children by herself,' said Lou.

'She's got help,' said Patrick unsympathetically. 'She got the house and she'll have someone to clean it and an au pair to take care of the kids. She doesn't even have to work. And when it comes down to it, it was her choice.'

'It's tiring bringing up children,' said Lou, although she was feeling less sympathetic since hearing about the cleaner and the au pair and the lack of a mortgage.

A cleaner, imagine it! Imagine having a house with no rent or mortgage to pay. Even better. She'd hold on the au pair though. Grace would make mincemeat of the poor girl.

'Kids can be very consuming,' she said.

'I know,' said Patrick. 'That's precisely why I've chosen not to have them. You can keep all your dirty nappies and your grazed knees and your adolescent tantrums. I don't want to be bothered with any of that.'

'But are you any happier than Catriona?'

'Of course I am!'

Lou looked unconvinced. 'You say she's not happy, but I bet she is. I bet she doesn't regret having those children for an *instant*. Of course it's hard work. There are days when I'm so exhausted just getting through the day, and it all seems a never-ending battle, and then I'll look at the back of Tom's neck, or hear Grace laughing, and they're so…*miraculous*…I feel like my heart's going to stop with the sheer joy of them. Do you ever feel like that?'

'I do when I look at my Porsche,' said Patrick flippantly.

'Enough to make up for a failed marriage and losing your wife?'

'Look, I was bitter when Catriona left. Of course I was,' he said, a slightly defensive edge to his voice. 'I'm not going to pretend I've been ecstatically happy all the time, ever since, but I've moved on. I've been successful in a way I would never have dreamed of when I was married to Catriona. I've built up some great companies, and I've made lots of money while I was at it. I've worked hard and I've had a good life. And I've got the kind of car most men can only fantasise about.'

'Oh, well, as long as you've got a nice *car*…'

'You may mock, but it means a lot.'

'I think you may need to be a man to understand that one,' said Lou. Tom and Lawrie certainly would.

'Let's put it this way,' said Patrick, pointing a fork at her for emphasis. 'I can do what I want. I can go where I want, when I want, with whoever I want. You don't think that makes me happy?'

'Right.' Lou nodded understandingly as she buttered another piece of bread. She hoped the food was coming soon. She was starving. 'So when was the last time you went away? You certainly haven't been anywhere in the last three months.'

'I've been busy, in case you hadn't noticed,' said Patrick, thrown off balance by this new, combative Lou. 'I had a company to save!'

'Hey, we managed for years before you came along! We wouldn't have fallen apart if you'd taken a long weekend. You didn't even go away at Easter. Don't you ever wish that you were working for something more than to make more money? That you had someone to go home to at the end of the day?'

'Aren't you trying to ask me if I ever get lonely?' said Patrick sardonically.

'Well, don't you?'

'I don't need to be on my own if I don't choose to. I've had plenty of relationships, and I'm not short of female company.'

So Lou had gathered from the gossip columns.

Perhaps it was just as well that the food arrived before she had time to frame a tart retort. Patrick had to watch while Lou went through her smiling routine again, and the waiter, this one old enough to have known better, fell over himself to serve her. He picked up her napkin, refilled both of her glasses, offered to fetch her more bread and ground pepper from an extremely suggestive-looking mill.

Extraordinary, thought Patrick. He studied her across the table. She had taken off her jacket and was wearing a simple, silky sort of top with a scoop neck, its plainness set off by a striking silver necklace. OK, she was elegant in a classic way and she had a charming smile—it seemed to work on waiters and barmen, anyway—but there wasn't anything particularly special about the rest of her.

Well, she had nice eyes, he supposed, amending his opinion slightly, and all the assurance of an older woman, but there was no way you could describe her as beautiful. Not like Ariel, who had all the bloom and radiance of youth. Still, now that he was looking at her properly, he could see that she *did* have a certain allure with that dark hair and those dark eyes.

Funny, this was the first time he had really been aware of her as a woman. He must have seen the line of her throat and the curve of her mouth almost every day for the last three months, and yet tonight was the first time he had noticed them at all.

Patrick frowned slightly. He wasn't sure he really wanted to start noticing things like that about Lou. There was something vaguely unsettling about thinking of her as a woman, warm and real, as opposed to the impersonal PA who ran his office so efficiently. About realising how oddly the generous curve of her lips sat with that air of cool competence or the ironic undertone in her voice sometimes.

And there was something *very* unsettling about noticing the way that top shifted as she leant forward to pick up her glass. The material seemed to slither over her skin, and it was impossible not to wonder how it would feel beneath his hands, how warm and smooth her body would be underneath…

Patrick looked abruptly away. Enough of that.

'What about you?' he said, struggling to remember what they had been talking about. She had been making him cross, and that was good. Anything was better than watching that top slip and slide as she breathed. 'Are you Mrs Happy?'

'I think I'm pretty happy,' she said, swirling the wine in her glass as she considered the matter. 'Content, anyway. I'm not joyously happy the way I was when I was first married, and when Grace and Tom were babies, but I've got a lot to be happy about. My children are healthy, I've got a dear aunt who's like a mother to me, I've got good friends... It's just a shame about my awful job. I've got this boss who makes my life an absolute misery.'

'What?' Patrick did a double take. He had been so busy not noticing what was going on with that damn top—why couldn't the woman sit still, for God's sake?—that it took him a moment to realise what she had said.

'That was a joke,' said Lou patiently.

'Oh. Right.' Patrick was surprised by how relieved he felt. 'Ha, ha,' he said morosely, and then was startled when Lou laughed. She had a proper laugh, not a giggle or a simper, and it made her look younger, vibrant, interesting, really quite...*sexy*. Was that what the waiter had seen too?

'Sorry,' she said. 'Just checking to see if you were listening!'

Patrick had the alarming feeling that things were slipping out of control and he got a grip of himself with an effort. There must have been something very odd in that champagne. He wasn't feeling like himself at all.

'You're on your own, though.' That was better; think of her as a sad divorcee. 'Don't *you* get lonely?'

'When you live in a tiny flat with two growing children, I can tell you that you long for the chance to be lonely sometimes!' said Lou.

'That's not what I mean, and you know it,' he said.

'No, OK,' she acknowledged. 'I miss being married sometimes,' she said slowly, pushing her plate aside so that she could lean her arms on the table and prop her face in one palm, oblivious to what that did to her cleavage, or what the effect on Patrick might be.

'It's hard bringing up children on your own,' she told him, while he fought to concentrate. 'There's no one to talk to in the evening, no one to share your worries with, no one who cares the way you do about their little triumphs.'

She was gazing at the candle flame, miles away with her children, and Patrick wondered if she had forgotten that he was there. If she had, he didn't like it, he realised.

'It would just be nice sometimes to have someone to support you when everything seems to be going wrong,' she said.

'Someone to hold you?' he suggested, his voice harder than he had intended, and Lou's dark eyes flashed up from the candle to meet his for a taut moment while both of them tried not to think about being held.

Her gaze dropped first. 'Yes, someone to hold me,' she said quietly. 'Sometimes.'

Patrick had a sudden memory of Lou walking across the lobby earlier that evening. She had seemed so prim and proper then, so cool and composed. Not appealing at all. He was almost appalled to realise how warm and soft and inviting she looked now, her eyes dark, gleaming pools in the candlelight, and her hair just a little tousled. He wondered what it would be like to touch it, to run his fingers through it and let the dark, silky strands fall back against her cheek.

What had happened? Then the neat suit and the demure top had struck him as merely dull. Now they seemed tantalising, as if they were specifically designed to make him wonder what she might be wearing underneath. If she were warm and willing in his lap, would he be able to slide his hand over her knee and under that businesslike skirt and discover that she was wearing stockings?

Patrick swallowed. God, he had to stop this right now. Talk about inappropriate. He didn't want Lou to think that he was just another lecherous businessman fantasising about secretaries in tight skirts and stockings and high heels.

Although if the cap fitted...

Picking up his glass, he took a gulp of wine and made a sterling effort to pull himself together.

'Yes, being held...I do miss that,' Lou was saying thoughtfully, unaware of Patrick's confusion. 'I think what I miss most, though, is the feeling that you don't have to deal with *everything* on your own, that someone is interested in you for yourself, and not just because you're a mother and there to be taken for granted. I don't mind when the kids do that, I know that's part of their job, but still...'

She glanced at him, evidently hesitating, and Patrick cleared his throat and nodded encouragingly.

'Go on, tell me. This is confession time, remember? Nothing to be remembered or held against you tomorrow!'

Lou laughed in spite of herself. 'OK, then, but you get to tell me an embarrassing fantasy too.'

'It's a fantasy? Better and better!'

A slight blush crept up her cheeks, but she hoped the candlelight would disguise it. 'Mine's not a very exciting fantasy, I'm afraid. I imagine that I can skip the awkwardness of meeting a man, dating him, getting to know him, all of that. I don't want the falling-in-love bit again. It's too consuming, and it hurts too much when you lose it.'

'So where does the fantasy come in?'

'I just want to wake up and find myself comfortably married to someone,' she confessed. 'Someone nice and...*kind*. Someone I could lean on when I needed to, and support when he needed it, and the rest of the time we'd be...I don't know...friends, I suppose.'

'What's embarrassing about that?' asked Patrick, his mind straying distractingly back to Lou's stockings. If they *were* stockings. He really, really wanted to know now.

Could he ask her? Patrick wondered, and then caught himself. What was he *thinking* of? Of course he couldn't ask his PA if she was wearing stockings. That would be sexual harassment.

'It's so politically incorrect,' said Lou guiltily. 'I'm a strong, independent woman. I shouldn't need anyone to look after me. I can look after myself. And I do, most of the time,' she said, recovering herself. 'I only think about having someone else when I'm tired, or feeling down, or one of the kids is being difficult.'

Which was a depressing number of times in the week, when she thought about it.

'It doesn't sound to me like an impossible fantasy,' said Patrick carefully. 'You'll just have to keep an eye out for someone suitable.'

'Oh, yes, and there are so many kind, supportive, single men out there!'

'There must be someone,' said Patrick. 'You're an attractive woman.' Rather too attractive for his own comfort, it appeared.

'I'm also forty-five and have two bolshy adolescents who consume every moment I'm not at work,' she pointed out. 'Would you want to take that on?'

'Not when you put it like that.'

'There isn't any other way to put it,' said Lou. 'I've been divorced over six years now, and I've learnt to cope on my own. I'm not looking for a man.'

'I've heard that before,' said Patrick cynically, thinking of the women who had assured him that they were just out for a good time and then started dawdling past jewellers' windows and dropping heavy hints about moving in with him.

This was good. He wasn't thinking about stockings any more.

Much.

'It's true.' Lou fixed him with one of her disconcertingly direct looks. 'Frankly, I haven't got the energy to put into finding a man, let alone maintaining a relationship. When you work all day, and go home to two children who need all your attention, it's hard to imagine being with anyone new.'

'And even if I did by some remote chance meet someone who didn't mind only meeting every few weeks when I could persuade a friend to babysit, and wasn't put off by Grace's moods, or the fact that I don't have a bedroom of my own, and was happy with only ever getting the fraction of my attention that was left over from my children, I'd still hesitate,' she said. 'It's taken me a long time to build up my life again after Lawrie left. I'm not going to let it all come crashing down in smithereens like before.'

'You mean if you were hurt again?' said Patrick.

'Yes. I won't expose myself to it.' Draining her glass, Lou set it down firmly in front of her, absolutely definite.

'So you won't even take a risk?'

'If it was just me, maybe I would,' she said, and then thought about the pain and the heartache she'd been through. 'Maybe. But I've got two children who were caught in the fallout of a failed relationship. I won't do that to them again. Anyway,' she said, going on the counter-attack, 'I notice you haven't rushed to remarry either!'

'No, once was enough for me,' Patrick agreed. 'I wasn't good at being married. I hated the endless negotiations and guessing games.'

'It doesn't have to be like that,' Lou pointed out. There

had never been any question of negotiating with Lawrie. He had gone his own charming way without ever considering that she might be affected by what he was doing.

'No, but it often is. Every relationship I've had since my divorce has been the same. The thing about women is that they're never satisfied. You give them what they ask for, and then they want more.'

'I don't think that's very fair,' said Lou, trying to remember the last time she'd been given what she asked for by a man.

'Isn't it?' Patrick demanded. He was feeling more himself now. Good. The stockings thing had obviously just been a momentary aberration.

He leant forward, counting off the points on his fingers. 'You're getting on well and having a good time together, but then they want to leave their hair-dryer or something at your house. Just something small to stake a claim on your space. They want you to say you love them, and when you say you love them, they want commitment. And when you've committed yourself, they want you to move in with them, or marry them, and then they want babies...

'And those are just the big things,' he said. 'At the same time they're working on you to change your life completely, they want you to understand them and talk to them and surprise them with little presents and weekends away. They want you to send them flowers and emails and to ring them from work so they know that you're thinking about them the whole time. I tell you, it's never-ending demands with women.'

He drained his glass morosely. 'Basically they want to take over your whole life.'

Lou was unimpressed by his suffering. 'So what you're saying is that you want to have sex but you don't want a relationship?'

'What's the big deal about relationships anyway?' Patrick grumbled. 'Women are obsessed with them! I thought I might get on better if I dated younger women. I figured they'd be happy to have a good time and not care about settling down, but, oh, no! We've only been out a couple of times and they're talking about *our relationship*.'

He sighed. 'Before you know where you are, you're in the middle of all that emotional hassle again.'

'It must be awful for you,' said Lou, not bothering to hide her sarcasm.

Patrick shot her a look. 'Why do women *do* that?' he complained.

'Well, you see, we tend to have these awkward things called feelings,' Lou explained with mock patience. 'It's annoying of us, I know, but there's nothing we can do about it. We *will* go and fall in love without thinking about how tedious it is for you to have someone who adores you and will do anything for you.'

She shook her head in pretended disbelief. 'I mean, how selfish is *that*?'

'I'm serious,' said Patrick. 'I just wish I could find a woman who was happy to take things as they are without always fretting about the future or what it all means or what will happen between us. As it is, we only go out for a few weeks before she starts to get clingy and I start to get claustrophobic.'

He grimaced. 'The thought of tying myself down for life is too horrible to contemplate. I'd be bored within a month.'

'You didn't get bored with Catriona,' Lou pointed out.

Patrick thought about living with Catriona. They had both been so young and excited to be living together. They had argued a lot, but it hadn't been boring. He had missed her when she had gone.

'That was different.'

'How?'

Patrick wished that Lou would stop asking difficult questions. 'It just was,' he said.

'Nothing to do with the fact that you and Catriona were the same age, and now you're twice as old as any girl you might contemplate marrying?'

And she could stop putting her finger on the nub of the matter while she was at it.

'No.' He scowled at her. 'It's just that the older I get, the more I value my freedom. I like my life as it is. I work hard, I play hard and if I find a woman attractive, I can do something about it.'

Although clearly that wasn't always the case, he added mentally, remembering Lou's stockings.

Damn. Patrick cursed inwardly. He was supposed to have forgotten about them.

'That's not to say it wouldn't be very handy to have a wife sometimes,' he said, pushing the stockings to the back of his mind once more. 'It would be good to have someone who could deal with the domestic and social side of things. I can't be bothered with all of that, but there are times when I have to entertain and it would all be a lot easier if I were married.'

'You can always have a housekeeper to take care of the house, and there must be any number of caterers falling over themselves to cook for people like you.'

'Quite. That's exactly what I do at the moment. But it's not quite the same as having a hostess who can welcome people and introduce them to each other and do all the chit-chat.'

'Have you ever tried any of your girlfriends?'

'No.' Patrick looked horrified. 'It's bad enough taking them along to receptions and parties. They're not interested in business. They get bored and end up more of a liability than an asset. I can just imagine what would happen if I asked them to help me entertain business associates to dinner. That would be *commitment.*' He sneered the word. 'They'd be off buying wedding magazines the next day.'

'I can't believe that all these girls are really that desperate to marry you,' said Lou, exasperated by his attitude. 'It's not like you're *that* big a deal.'

Of course, incredibly wealthy, single, intelligent men in their forties weren't that easy to come by, she had to admit. And it wasn't as if Patrick were grotesquely ugly, either. He probably had a pretty fair notion of how attractive he was.

Not her type of course. The cockiness of Tom Cruise and the cool of Clint Eastwood was how she had described him to Marisa. 'Tell me he's got the looks of George Clooney and I'll come and work for him myself!' Marisa had said.

But Patrick was no George Clooney. He was too cold, his features too austere. He had none of Lawrie's rakish good looks, or his easy charm, but still... Lou considered him anew. There was something *definite* about him, she decided, something solid and steady, and when he listened he concentrated completely on what you were saying. He looked at you properly, instead of letting his eyes wander around looking for something or someone more interesting the way Lawrie's had done.

Funny that she had never noticed that before, thought Lou. Or his mouth, so cool and firm and intriguing. The kind of mouth you couldn't help wondering about, how it would feel, how it would kiss. Not that she would want to, Lou reminded herself. It was just funny that she hadn't noticed it until now, that was all.

Funny to realise what a difference a gleam of humour

made, too, lightening his expression and warming the cold eyes.

Funny how his smile made her heart jump, just a little. Must be all that champagne she had drunk.

'Why don't you try going out with women who've got bigger ambitions?' she said, forcing her mind back to the subject at issue. 'Someone who's got a career of her own and who doesn't want to settle down any more than you do?'

'Believe me, I would if I could find a girl like that,' said Patrick. 'I might even be prepared to marry her.'

'What, and give up your precious freedom?'

'At least it would shut my mother up. She's constantly going on at me to get married again. She thinks it would be good for me to have someone else to think about. She says it would stop me being so selfish.'

He sounded aggrieved and Lou smothered a smile. She rather liked the idea of him having a mother who was no more impressed with him than his PA.

'Does she want grandchildren? Is that why she's keen for you to get married?'

'I think she's accepted that she's not going to get them from me,' he said, and pointed a finger at Lou's expression. 'Don't you go feeling sorry for her! She can't complain. She's already got eleven grandchildren. I'd have thought that was more than enough.'

'Eleven?' said Lou, trying to adjust to the idea of Patrick as part of a large family.

'I've got three sisters, all of whom seem to be very fertile, and all of whom also think I should get married. Every time I see them, they ask me what's the point of having all that money and not enjoying it. Just because they've got big families of their own, they think I should have that too,' he grumbled.

'I tell them I'm perfectly happy living on my own, and I am, but sometimes when I go home the house *does* seem a bit empty,' he admitted, and gave a rather shamefaced smile. 'There, that's my embarrassing confession!'

'That's a confession, not a fantasy,' said Lou light-heartedly.

She was feeling extraordinarily mellow. It was oddly comfortable to be sitting here with him, talking to Patrick about things she would never normally *dream* of discussing with anyone at work, let alone her boss, talking to him as if he were a friend.

It was strange now to think that she had been perfectly happy to have a cool working relationship with him. For a fleeting moment, Lou wondered whether she would regret her confidences in the morning, but she pushed the thought aside. She would just blame it on the champagne.

Not to mention the wine. They seemed to have made major inroads into that bottle in spite of her plans to stick to the occasional sip.

She wasn't going to worry about it now, anyway. She was here, away from home, away from the children. It was like being in a bubble, time out from the day-to-day reality of commuting and cooking and preparing lunchboxes. Everything felt different.

Patrick even *looked* different. Warmer somehow, more human, more approachable. Much more attractive than he should for a man who wasn't her type, anyway.

'Go on,' she told him. 'You said it was confession time, and that we'd forget it all tomorrow. I told you my fantasy, so I think you should tell me yours.'

Patrick thought about leaning over the table and whispering that she should forget pudding, that he wanted to take her upstairs and press her against the bedroom door, that he wanted to explore the back of her knee while he kissed her, to let his hand smooth insistently up her thigh, pushing up that prim little skirt until his fingers found the top of her stocking, and then—

'One of them anyway,' said Lou, unnerved by the way his eyes had darkened. She didn't know what he was thinking about just then, but she was pretty sure it would leave her blushing.

And more than a little jealous. There had been something in his expression that had made her pulse kick in a way it hadn't for a very long time. Now was not the time for it to start doing that, and her boss was not the man to set it off either. Whatever he had been fantasising about doing with one of those blonde stick insects he liked so much, she didn't want to hear it.

'A fantasy that will embarrass you, not me,' she specified firmly.

It was just as well she had said that, thought Patrick, a mixture of amusement and horror at the narrowness of his escape tugging at the corner of his mouth. For a minute there he had got a bit carried away. Fortunately, her intervention had given him time to unscramble his brains. Reality had slotted back into place and all the disadvantages of explaining to your PA that you were fantasising about her and her choice of lingerie had presented themselves starkly.

Not a good idea, in fact.

'OK...' he said, drawing out the syllables. He drank some wine while he tried to focus. Surely he could think of something to tell her? A fantasy...a fantasy...and keep right away from stockings...

'Right,' he said after a moment. 'Well, how about this one? It's not that different from yours, actually. What I'd really like is all the advantages of marriage without any of the drawbacks. So in my fantasy, I would have a wife who was there when I needed her. She would be the perfect hostess, remember all my sisters' birthdays, and mysteriously vanish whenever I met a new and beautiful girl so that I could continue to have guilt-free affairs.'

Lou rolled her eyes, unimpressed. 'Oh, the old fantastic-sex-without-a-relationship chestnut! I don't think that's like my fantasy *at all*,' she objected. 'But I can see why it appeals to you.'

Patrick wasn't quite sure how to take that. 'Well, since it's likely to remain a fantasy, I'll reconcile myself to an empty house, to hiring caterers and disappointing my mother.'

Thinking about it, Lou absently held out her glass for another refill.

'What you really need,' she said, 'is someone who's prepared to marry you for your money, and treat marriage like a job.'

'That's not very romantic!'

'You don't need romance,' she told him sternly. 'You need someone to run your house, to be your social secretary, to be pleasant and interested when you go out as a couple but turn a blind eye to your affairs and generally expect absolutely nothing from you other than access to your bank account.'

Patrick was impressed by her assessment and said so as he topped up her glass. 'That's exactly what I need.'

'In fact,' said Lou, 'you need to marry me.'

CHAPTER THREE

PATRICK'S hand jerked and he missed her glass, spilling wine on the tablecloth. 'Sorry,' he said as he mopped it up with his napkin. 'I thought you said that I should marry you there!'

'I did.' Lou accepted her glass back with a smile of thanks, quite unfazed. 'Someone like me, anyway. But actually, now I come to think of it, I'd be the perfect wife for you.'

'You would?' Patrick wasn't sure whether to be amused or appalled.

'Of course.' Lou gestured grandly with her glass. 'I know your business, and I could do all that social stuff easily. I know who you need to charm and who to impress, and I'm under absolutely no illusions as to what you're like!'

'Right,' said Patrick, fascinated.

'You'd be much better off with someone sensible like me who wouldn't make a fuss about your girlfriends, or expect you to pay me any attention,' she pointed out. 'You wouldn't need to email me every day or buy me flowers or surprise me with mini-breaks to Paris.'

'O...K,' he said slowly, buying time until he worked out whether she was joking or not. 'But why would you want to marry me?'

'Oh, I'd be marrying you for your money, of course,' said Lou cheerfully.

'I thought you didn't want a man?'

'I don't, but I do want financial security. Do you have

any idea how tough it is to be a single parent living on a limited income in a city like London?'

Patrick raised his brows. 'Is this a very roundabout way of complaining about your salary?'

'No.' She shook her head. 'My salary is fair. More than fair, in fact. If it wasn't, I would have got another job. It just doesn't go very far when you have to pay an extortionate rent and feed and support two growing children into the bargain.'

'Yes, I've heard that children are expensive nowadays,' said Patrick, thinking of his sisters' complaints.

'They are, and the older they are, the more expensive they seem to become.' Lou sighed and sipped her wine reflectively. 'I'd like to be able to say that I had raised a couple of thoughtful, unmaterialistic, community-minded children who understood that the love and security you strive to give them mattered more than the latest brand of trainers or the newest computer game, but sadly they're not like that at all!'

'Oh?' said Patrick, rather taken with the idea that Lou's children weren't the paragons he would have expected them to be. He found her attitude refreshing. He'd had to listen to too many mothers telling him how clever and talented and generally marvellous their children were.

'They're not bad kids,' said Lou, 'but they're like all their friends. They want to be in with the in-crowd, to be like everyone else and to have what everyone else has. At least I haven't been able to spoil them,' she added with a wry smile. 'The silver lining of living on a strict budget. Although naturally Grace and Tom don't see it that way!'

'Doesn't their father give you any financial support?' asked Patrick, ever the businessman. As a man who specialised in taking failing businesses and turning them round, he was clearly offended by the idea of losing control of your finances.

Lou sighed a little, thinking of Lawrie. 'He's always willing in principle, but when it comes to transferring money there's always some great scheme that he needs to buy into temporarily which will solve all our problems.'

'And does it?'

'No. The last time he had any real money to invest, he lost us our house,' said Lou, trying to make light of it. 'There's no way I'm getting back on the property ladder in London now.'

'Unfortunate,' commented Patrick, looking disapproving. He was far too canny a businessman ever to take the kind of risks Lawrie ran all the time.

Lou thought of the day Lawrie had come home and confessed that he had borrowed against the house, and lost it all on some idiotic venture that a child of six could have told him would fail.

Oh, and that by the way he was leaving her for a younger, prettier woman who wasn't so boring about being sensible about money.

Of course, the other woman didn't have two children to worry about, so it was easy for her.

Lou had lost her home and her husband on a single day. A double whammy as her world fell apart. Not one of the best days of her life.

'It was a bit,' she agreed, smiling bitterly at the understatement.

There was a pause. Patrick was having to adjust his ideas about Lou. She had always seemed so cool and in control, it was hard to imagine her dragged down by a feckless husband, having to scrape and make do.

'So marrying for money might solve some of your problems?' he said, trying to lighten the atmosphere, and Lou was glad to follow his lead.

'Well, I've got to admit that I haven't given it a lot of thought as an option before,' she said, 'but I really think it might. In fact, I wonder if marrying you might not be just the thing!'

'I'm glad you think I might be of some use to you!'

'When you're in my position, you can't afford to be proud,' said Lou frankly. 'I'm sick of scraping by and worrying about money the whole time. And I hate not being able to give Grace and Tom the kind of life I want for them.'

'You said you didn't want to give them things,' Patrick reminded her, and she nodded.

'I don't. They don't need things, but they do need more space, for instance. If you saw where we live now…'

She trailed off with a grimace at the thought of the flat. 'I know we're better off than some, but it's a tiny apartment for the three of us. Grace and I have to share a bedroom, and Tom's is barely more than a cupboard. If you want to have any privacy, you have to go into the bathroom, and even then there's always one of them banging on the door.'

Lou sighed. 'It's so small we all get on top of each other, and that makes everyone scratchy. I'm sure we wouldn't argue nearly so much if we had more space.' She cocked her head at him. 'You've got a big house, haven't you?'

'I've got three.'

'There you go, then. Plenty of room to spread ourselves. And I bet you don't have neighbours going through a marital crisis on one side of you, while those on the other put the television on full blast at seven in the morning and don't turn it off until well after midnight?'

'I don't know what state my neighbours' marriage is in,

or what their viewing habits are, but I certainly can't hear them,' agreed Patrick.

'I didn't think so. And you probably don't have people upstairs either?'

'No, I've got the whole house to myself.'

Lou sighed enviously. 'Our neighbours upstairs are perfectly nice, but every footstep reverberates through the ceiling, and we can hear almost everything they say above a whisper.'

'It sounds as if marrying me would certainly improve your accommodation prospects,' said Patrick dryly.

'Oh, don't worry, I'd want your money too.' Lou waved a piece of bread at him gaily. 'Not millions, just enough to be able to do the kind of things I could have done for them if Lawrie had stayed and we hadn't lost the house. I'd love to be in a position where I could encourage their interests, give them a chance to develop their talents, open their eyes to how other people live…'

She trailed off wistfully. 'I'd really like to be able to take them abroad for a holiday one year. Grace has friends whose father took them to the States last summer. They had a week in Florida, and a week in New York, where they stayed in some swish apartment and got taken round the Statue of Liberty in a private speedboat. Grace was so jealous, she could hardly speak to Alice and Harriet when they got back. I know she'd love a holiday like that, but all I can afford is to take them to see my aunt in the Yorkshire Dales. It's not that exciting for a fourteen-year-old.'

It didn't sound that exciting to a forty-eight-year-old either, thought Patrick, and then sucked in an exasperated breath as he saw the waiters bearing down on them once more with their main courses. They had to go through the whole rigmarole as before, both waiters hovering sycophantically around Lou and vying to top up her glass or express the hope that she would enjoy her meal.

And Lou just sat there, encouraging them with that smile of hers.

Patrick watched them grovel off at last with a disgruntled expression. 'If things are that tight, wouldn't it be cheaper for you to move out of London?'

'Yes, I often think that,' said Lou as she picked up her knife and fork. 'It's the rent that's so expensive anywhere within commuting distance of London. I'd love to live in the country, and I'm sure I could get some kind of job, although it's not easy starting in a new place when you're over forty.'

'So why don't you do it?'

'Because the kids would hate it. They're both settled at a good school in the centre of London. London's all they've ever known, so they're real metropolitans now. It's bad enough taking them to the Dales for a week. They just droop around and say that they're bored. Tom's not too bad when you get him up and out, but Grace pines for her friends.'

'You can't arrange your whole life around your children,' said Patrick, looking down his nose disapprovingly.

Lou put down her knife and fork and looked at him in wonder at his lack of understanding. 'But that's *exactly* what you have to do,' she corrected him. 'That's the thing about having children. They always come first.

'And the fact is that Grace and Tom would be miserable living in the country now,' she went on, picking up her cutlery once more so that she could tuck into her meal. 'All their friends are in London. That's their home. They're used to taking the tube and jumping on and off buses.

'No,' she said with mock resolution. 'It's a choice between marrying you or winning the lottery.'

Patrick was enjoying Lou's novel approach. Not that he had any real intention of getting married, but at least her frankness about his money made a change from tears and protestations of love and tedious conversations about why he wasn't prepared to commit.

'Let's just say for the sake of argument that I did marry you,' he said. 'How would it work?'

'It would be a meeting of our two fantasies,' said Lou, warming to the idea. 'We wouldn't have to pretend to be in love or any of that nonsense. I'd do the dutiful-wife act. I'd run your house, turn up for business dos and remind you to ring your mother, but other than that you'd hardly know I was there. You could chase girls all you liked and I wouldn't be the slightest bit jealous. I'd just wave you off, tell you to have a nice time and remind you to leave me your credit card!'

She laughed at the absurdity of the idea. Honestly, she must have had far too much to drink, but she was at the merry stage where she couldn't bring herself to care.

Patrick was having a bit of trouble disentangling the fantasies they had discussed from the one they definitely hadn't. Clearly, Lou wasn't talking about the one with the stockings, anyway. He'd certainly know she was there in that one.

With an effort he remembered what she had told him about her fantasy. Something about having someone to talk to, wasn't it? Nothing about stockings, that was for sure.

'So what would I have to do?'

Lou was enjoying herself. 'Oh, you'd just have to be there occasionally for me to have a moan about things, but it shouldn't cut into your seduction time too much. All I'd really want would be the run of the house and the security of knowing I wasn't going to find myself homeless again.'

'Does that mean if it was all a disaster and we ended up getting divorced I'd have to give you my house?'

'Well, if you've got three, you could probably spare one,' said Lou frankly. 'It doesn't seem very fair though, I agree.'

She pondered the matter, her brows drawn together in concentration as she continued to sip her wine absently. 'I'm sure we could draw up some kind of pre-nuptial contract. You know, like they do in Hollywood. We'd just put in some clause that said you had to give me some money if you got fed up of me,' she decided.

'But, hey, why would you want to divorce me?' Lou went on breezily. 'A marriage of convenience would solve all your problems. In fact, we'd both get exactly what we wanted.'

'Right,' said Patrick, a grin twitching at the corner of his mouth. 'Remind me again where our fantasies collide.'

'I want financial security. You want sex without commitment. Honestly, it's ideal,' said Lou. 'We would both know exactly where we were. There'd be no question of falling in love, or any of those messy emotions you're so afraid of. I don't want to get involved any more than you do.'

Patrick studied her with amusement. She had obviously had even more champagne than he had. He had the feeling that they would both regret this conversation in the morning, but for now he was finding it very entertaining.

'So you think you're the ideal wife for me?'

'I do,' she said with owlish dignity. 'I'm offering you a great deal here!'

'What about the two stroppy adolescents that come with you?'

'Yes, I'm afraid that Grace and Tom would come as part of the package, and I can see that they could be a bit of a drawback from your point of view,' Lou conceded, determined to be fair. 'But you did say that your house feels empty sometimes, and they would fill it up nicely. I presume you've got bedrooms for us all?'

Patrick did a quick calculation. 'Six.'

'Six?' She paused for a moment to consider how much a six-bedroom house in Chelsea must be worth. The answer made her mind boggle, and she shook her head.

'What on earth were you doing buying a house with six bedrooms when you live on your own?'

'It had good off-road parking.'

He sounded quite serious, too.

'Well, it's high time you filled up some of those rooms, if you ask me,' she said, recovering her nerve. 'It sounds excellent for us. There would be plenty of room for the kids to spread themselves, and we can all have a room each, *and* have two spare for visitors.'

'Oh, so you and I wouldn't be sharing a room, then?' said Patrick, having worked out the bedroom allocation.

Dark eyes met his squarely across the table. 'Not as long as you're sleeping around,' she said.

Ah. Not quite *that* intoxicated, then, thought Patrick.

'Some wife you'd be,' he pretended to grumble.

'You don't want to sleep with me,' Lou pointed out, 'and I certainly don't want to sleep with you!'

So much for his stockings fantasy. 'Well, that seems clear enough.' Patrick knew that she was right, but couldn't quite prevent the slight edge to his voice.

Lou heard it, and realised belatedly that she hadn't been very flattering. 'That's not to say that you're unattractive,' she tried to reassure him, even as part of her wondered why she was bothering to prop an ego that was already quite big enough. 'In fact, you're much more attractive than I thought you were.'

Oh, God, she'd had far too much to drink! She hadn't meant to say that at all. 'When I said I didn't want to sleep with you, I didn't mean...at least, I *did* mean... Well, I was just trying to say that it's not that—'

She stopped abruptly. There was no way that sentence was going anywhere she wanted it to, so she might as well give up on it now.

'I know what you meant,' said Patrick, keeping his face straight with difficulty. 'I think! I can see it would still be a pretty good deal for me,' he added, taking pity on Lou's confusion.

'It would be.' She beamed at him, grateful for rescuing her from the great big hole she had dug for herself there. She picked up her glass. 'You should think about it.'

Patrick looked at her, pink-cheeked and distinctly dishevelled by now. He could hardly recognise his prim and proper PA.

'Maybe I should.'

Lou stared fixedly at the lift button and tried not to sway. Really, she must have drunk more than she thought.

'I don't usually drink this much,' she confided to Patrick, with the nasty feeling that she was slurring her words. Getting to her feet had been more difficult than it usually was, too, and the walk across the hotel lobby to the lifts had involved a lot more concentration than it should have done.

'Honestly, no one would ever guess,' he said, and grinned. 'Perhaps I'd better see you to your room!'

Lou thought about walking along the dimly lit hotel corridor to her bedroom with him by her side, thought about saying goodnight. With anyone else, she wouldn't hesitate about kissing them on the cheek to thank them for dinner, but Patrick wasn't anyone else. She couldn't imagine kissing him.

Or was that quite true? Perversely, her mind proceeded to imagine it perfectly well. With unnerving clarity, in fact. Lou saw herself leaning in to brush his cheek with her lips and breathe in the smell of male skin and clean shirt, saw the corner of Patrick's mouth curve into that smile she had been noticing all evening as he turned his head slightly and his lips met hers.

Uh-oh. Lou was dismayed to discover that her subconscious had been working on this for some time. Evidently it had already thought about *exactly* what his kiss would feel like, had spent some time calculating the way her bones would melt and her lips would part at the surge of pleasure at his touch, so it was all there for her to imagine, ready prepared.

She would be able to press into him, to wrap her arms around his lean, hard body and kiss him back while he tugged her top free and slid his hands under the silk and—

Good grief, what was she *doing*? Lou sucked in a deep breath as if surfacing after a dive and tried to still her hammering heart. Suddenly her body was humming, her mouth dry, and there didn't seem to be enough oxygen in the air. She was terrified to look at Patrick in case her thoughts were plastered all over her face.

Lou's cheeks burned. This was *it*. She was never touching alcohol again.

Where was the lift? Please, please, hurry up, Lou prayed.

As if catching her impatience, Patrick leant forward and jabbed impatiently at the button again. 'What are they doing—cranking the thing up and down by hand?' he asked irritably.

Lou didn't feel that an answer was expected, which was

just as well, given the extraordinary shortage of breath in her lungs right now.

In spite of herself, her eyes slid sideways to where Patrick was standing, looking conventional and utterly devastating in a suit, blue shirt and dark blue tie. The mere sight of him was enough to make her senses snarl with longing, to make her hands itch with the need to reach out and touch him, to make her throb with wanting to crawl all over him.

And she didn't even like the man!

Or she hadn't at the beginning of the evening, anyway.

Lou swallowed desperately and willed the lift to appear. This was *awful*. She didn't feel like herself *at all*. She just hoped the feeling would go away as soon as the alcohol had worn off. The sooner she got to bed—alone!—and had a good night's sleep, the better.

Ping. At last! The lift doors slid open and Patrick stood aside to let Lou in first. She walked primly past him, being very careful not to touch him and stood pressed against the back wall so that there was no chance of accidentally brushing against him. The way she felt, she wouldn't put it past herself to burst into flames, and then there really *would* be a nasty mess.

'Which floor?' asked Patrick as the doors began to close.

Oh, God, she wasn't up to answering questions that involved thinking! 'Um…four, I think.'

He turned from the control panel to look at her in surprise. 'You don't sound very sure. Do you know your room number?'

'Of course,' said Lou, flustered. 'It's…it's…' She dug around in her bag for the key card, but typically it wasn't marked with anything useful like a number. 'Four O seven,' she remembered with a gasp, and Patrick shot her a curious glance as he pressed the button marked four, and five for his own room, which was on the floor above.

Of course the lift *would* have to be empty, thought Lou bitterly. Had it been this small on the way down? There wasn't really *room* for two people, she decided, sucking in her stomach in a vain attempt to make more space between them. Patrick seemed to be very *close* somehow. How was she supposed to stop her hands grabbing for him when he was only inches away?

She clutched her bag to her chest to keep them under control.

Silence. It seemed to thrum in the enclosed space and Lou gazed desperately at the numbers above the door as they slid slowly upwards. After talking non-stop all evening, she now couldn't think of a single thing to say, and it was a huge relief when the doors pinged once more.

'Um…well…thanks for a lovely evening,' she gasped as the doors opened. 'See you tomorrow.'

Edging round Patrick, she stumbled out. Thank God, for that. Now all she had to do was get herself to her room, close the door and hope against hope that this evening had never happened.

'Lou?'

She turned to see Patrick holding open the lift doors.

'This is only the second floor,' he explained kindly.

Lou looked around her. That would explain why nothing looked familiar then.

'Oh. Yes. How silly of me.'

Mortified, she got back into the lift. Her face burned with embarrassment. Excellent. Here she was, aged forty-five, responsible mother of two and top-flight PA, making a complete and utter fool of herself.

'Here's four,' said Patrick as the doors sighed open once

more. 'Are you sure you don't need me to see you to your room after all?'

Lou couldn't look at him, but she could hear that he was smiling. 'I don't think there's any need for that,' she said with as much dignity as she could muster, which wasn't much. 'I'm perfectly all right,' she said and promptly tripped on the edge of the lift, only just recovering herself before she fell flat on her face.

Great.

'Lou, are you OK?'

'I'm fine, fine.' Lou summoned a bright smile and straightened her jacket. 'Absolutely fine.'

A smile hovered around Patrick's mouth, but she had to give him credit for not laughing out loud. 'Well, goodnight, then.' He released the doors and they closed slowly.

'Goodnight,' said Lou just in time as Patrick disappeared from view.

It took her ages to get the stupid card to release the lock on the door, but finally she made it into her room, kicked off her shoes and flopped onto the bed.

Could it really only be eleven o'clock? Lou peered at her watch. It had taken her just over three hours to ruin her image and probably destroy her career in the process. She was going to write a stiff letter of complaint to the chairman of the east coast line, just as soon as her head stopped spinning.

If they hadn't cancelled all the trains because of one piddly little storm, she would have been safely home alone by now. She would still be thinking of Patrick Farr as an arrogant businessman with whom she needed to have a coolly polite working relationship, but in whom she otherwise had no interest at all.

Instead of which, she had talked to him and got drunk with him and confided her fantasies to him, and now she was stuck with *liking* him, dammit. She wasn't going to be stuck with finding him attractive, though, Lou reassured herself. That was definitely off the agenda come tomorrow.

She just wished she hadn't made such a fool of herself in front of him.

Pulling her mobile phone out of her bag abruptly, Lou rolled over onto her front. She needed advice and Marisa never went to bed before midnight.

'I think I've just asked my boss to marry me,' she said when Marisa answered the phone.

'This would be the boss who never asks you about your weekend and is rude and arrogant, and doesn't look a bit like George Clooney, is that right?' said Marisa, who never minded phone calls that began in mid-conversation.

'Yes, except I don't think that he's that bad.' Lou rolled back so that she could look up at the ceiling and remember Patrick's face and the look in his eyes when she had asked about his fantasy. A squirmy feeling shivered down her spine at the memory. 'He's OK when you get to know him.'

'OK is not good enough for you to marry,' said Marisa firmly. 'You deserve someone who is fantastic at the very least.'

'I don't want to marry him,' said Lou, suddenly realising the implications of what she'd been saying to Patrick in the restaurant.

'Then why did you ask him to marry you?' asked Marisa, not unreasonably.

'I didn't really ask him,' Lou tried to explain. 'He was just talking about the kind of wife he wanted, and I said he needed someone like me.'

'And he responded to that how?'

'He said he'd think about it.'

'He sounds a cold fish to me,' said Marisa.

'I don't think he is really. He seems cold, but actually I think he could be quite...well, *hot*...'

There was a pause. 'Have you been drinking?'

'A bit.'

'Louisa Dennison, I'm going to tell your children on you!'

'Oh, please don't,' she begged. 'They'll never let me forget it! How are they, anyway?' she asked belatedly, feeling like a bad mother for not asking about them first.

'Fine. Sound asleep, and don't change the subject,' said Marisa. 'I want to know what's going on with you and Patrick What's-his-name.'

'Nothing's going on. We just had dinner.'

'And a vat of wine and talked about getting married!'

Lou cringed at the memory. 'The thing is, do you think when I see him tomorrow morning that I should apologise?'

'What for?'

'For all that marriage thing. I might have got a bit carried away,' Lou remembered uncomfortably. 'I told him I would be the perfect wife for him.'

'More to the point, would he be a perfect husband for you?'

'Definitely not,' said Lou. 'Patrick likes his women a good twenty years younger, with perfect bodies and an allergy to commitment of any kind.'

'Ah, he's a man, then!'

'This is serious,' said Lou crossly. 'My job's at stake.'

'He's not going to sack you for getting a bit drunk in your own time,' Marisa pointed out. 'It's not as if you were offensive...were you?'

'Of course not!'

'Well, then, I wouldn't worry about it. It sounds as if he had a fair amount to drink as well, and if he's anything like the men I know, he'll have a built-in ability to wipe any conversation concerning marriage from his memory. He'll either ignore it completely, or say that was a jolly good idea of yours and why don't you get married after all?'

Lou was appalled at the thought. 'I wasn't being serious! I've got no intention of marrying again. Once was enough for me!'

'Shame,' said Marisa lightly. 'I saw this wonderful hat the other day. It would be perfect for your wedding.'

'Buy it and keep it for Grace's wedding,' said Lou. 'She'll be getting married long before me!'

Marisa just laughed. 'We'll see.'

CHAPTER FOUR

'I WAS wondering if you'd like me to find you a temporary assistant,' said Lou as she gathered up her notebook and stood up to go.

Patrick looked up over the rim of his glasses from the letter he was reading. 'What on earth for?'

'I've got a week's holiday booked at the end of May. I did tell you about it,' she added as she saw him about to object.

'I don't remember,' he said unhelpfully. 'Does it have to be the end of May? We'll be busy preparing for the Packenham contract then.'

'Yes, it does have to be then,' said Lou crisply. 'It's half-term, and I need to spend that time with my children. And don't start about what a liability children are,' she warned him as he opened his mouth. 'This is the first time I've needed time off, and I booked it at the beginning of the year. I don't think that's unreasonable.'

It wasn't, but Patrick didn't feel inclined to admit it. The truth was that he didn't like the thought of Lou not being there. He *needed* her to run the office. He wouldn't be able to find anything without her, he'd get over-committed and nothing would work properly.

And he was used to her now.

In a funny kind of way.

Patrick had wondered if things might have been awkward after that evening they had spent together in Newcastle, but, in spite of the fact that neither of them had alluded to their conversation that night, in many ways the atmosphere between them was much easier. It was hard to stay frosty, after all, when you'd talked and laughed and confided your fantasies to each other—although not all of them, in Patrick's case.

Of course, Lou had reverted to her crisp and efficient self the next morning, but Patrick was no longer intimidated by her. He had seen her tipsy. He had seen her fall out of the lift. She couldn't fool him now. He knew she wasn't the ice-cold superwoman she had once seemed. Now that he let himself notice the glint of dry humour in her face, the warmth in her smile, the ironic undertone in her voice.

Too often for his own peace of mind, in fact, Patrick found himself thinking about the contrast between his cool, practical PA and the warm, vibrant woman he had glimpsed as she'd leant across the restaurant table, her dark eyes bright and her face vivid.

I'd be the perfect wife for you, she had said.

It was nonsense, of course. If he ever contemplated marriage again, it would be to someone beautiful and passionate and sexy. He certainly wouldn't be tying himself down to a middle-aged mother of two, no matter how good her legs were.

And they *were* good. Patrick knew because every time she walked into his office he would find himself looking at them and remembering his fantasy about whether she was wearing stockings or not. Her legs were great, in fact. He couldn't believe that he hadn't noticed them before.

He knew it was pathetic. He knew it was politically incorrect and deeply inappropriate, and probably perverted, but once the thought had slipped into his head it was impossible to get rid of it. It wasn't that Patrick hadn't tried. Life would be a lot easier if he had been able to carry on thinking of her suits as dull and demure instead of sexy as hell, which was how they now seemed to him. He began to think that it would be easier if Lou turned up for work in a miniskirt and plunging top. The kind of thing Ariel wore, in fact.

It was getting too distracting, that was the trouble. Patrick decided to stop noticing anything. It wasn't as if he were sex-starved, after all. Ariel was much prettier than Lou. She had a much better body, even better legs. What was more, Ariel was concerned when he was in a bad mood. She didn't just lift an ironic eyebrow, the way Lou did. Ariel never made him feel a fool. She never said cutting things.

But, then, she never made him laugh either, or left the office feeling empty when she had gone in the evenings.

Now Lou was talking about being away all week!

'It'll be very inconvenient,' he grumbled.

'That's why I'm asking if you want me to arrange for someone to cover the office,' said Lou patiently.

Patrick scowled. 'It won't be the same,' he said. 'I can't be bothered to explain everything.'

'Well, you can always answer your own phone,' said Lou, unperturbed. 'Or take the week off yourself.'

'What?'

'Take the week off, have a holiday, relax,' she said, stopping just short of rolling her eyes, although she might as well not have bothered, Patrick thought. It was perfectly obvious that she was doing it mentally. 'Or would that be too much like having a good time?' she asked, quite unnecessarily, in his opinion.

'I'm perfectly capable of having a good time,' he said, stung.

Lou didn't say anything. She just raised her brows and smiled faintly, in that deeply annoying way she had.

'All right.' Provoked, Patrick took off his reading glasses

and threw them onto his desk. 'I'll take the week off as well. You can book it tomorrow.'

Lou was already at her desk when Patrick came in the next morning. Her heart had developed an exasperating habit of jolting at the sight of him, but at least it didn't show—at least, she hoped that it didn't. She worked hard to keep her expression as indifferent as ever.

It had been a huge relief when she had met Patrick in the lobby the morning after that night she had made such a fool of herself in Newcastle. As Marisa had predicted, he appeared to have wiped the whole incident from his memory.

'How's the head?' was all he had said.

Lou had grimaced. 'Not good,' she'd admitted.

'I don't feel so hot either, to tell you the truth,' Patrick had said.

And that was it.

Nothing more had been said, and gradually Lou had let herself relax. It had just been a silly evening. Patrick was obviously prepared to pretend that it had never happened at all, and that suited her fine. She had other things to worry about, like Grace's determination to have her nose pierced, and Tom's run-in with his English teacher. She would forget it.

Only it wasn't that easy to forget. Lou was uncomfortably aware of Patrick now in a way that she had never been before. It had been awful on the train. Sitting opposite him in the first-class carriage on their way back to London, she had kept noticing his hands, his mouth, the line of his jaw, the crease of concentration between his brows.

Once Patrick had glanced up and caught her watching him, and her heart had jerked at the keenness of his eyes. Flushing, she had looked away and cleared her throat as she'd held out some papers. 'You wanted those budget figures for last year...'

Since then it hadn't been too bad, though. Patrick had no shortage of faults to concentrate on, so Lou made herself notice his abruptness rather than his mouth, his impatience rather than the way his eyes glinted when he smiled.

It was fine. Lou decided that she had made quite enough of a fool of herself in Newcastle. She certainly wasn't going to make things worse by getting obsessed with a ruthless, workaholic boss who was fixated on younger women. Even if her heart did jump a bit when she saw him.

Patrick paused by her desk on his way to his office.

'You can book me a holiday when you've finished that,' he told her.

Lou looked up, thought about asking him if he had ever thought of learning the word *please* and decided against it when she saw his face. Most people managed to look happy or excited at the idea of a holiday, but obviously not Patrick Farr.

'You're going?' she said, a little surprised.

'It was your idea,' he reminded her grouchily.

'Well, I do tend to have good ones,' she said, composed.

There was a short silence while the memory of her idea that they get married shimmered in the air between them. Patrick didn't need to say anything. Lou knew perfectly well that he was thinking about it. A flush crept up her cheeks and her poise slipped a little.

'Sometimes,' she said.

Patrick's eyes gleamed. 'Get me flights to the Maldives and a hotel for that week you're away.'

Lou raised her brows at his choice of destination, but made a note. 'Where do you want to stay?'

'Wherever's best,' he said indifferently. He had picked

up a report from her desk and was leafing through it. 'Book a suite, or a cabin, or whatever it is everyone has out there.'

'Best for what? Best location, best food, most luxurious?'

'I don't know.' Patrick gestured irritably. 'The most expensive.'

'Right.' Lou set her jaw. 'I take it you're not travelling alone?'

'No.' He closed the report with a slap and dropped it back onto the pile. 'One of the tickets should be in the name of Ariel Harper.'

Ariel. How charming, thought Lou, teeth mentally gritted. No doubt Hazel in Finance would be able to supply a photo, but Lou would take a bet on Ariel being blonde and ethereal. Oh, and twenty-five, tops.

'Put it through on my personal account,' said Patrick, and was about to turn away when he caught the look on Lou's face. 'What?' he demanded.

'Nothing, I'm just surprised at your choice of destination,' said Lou. 'I can't imagine you lying on a beach for a week.'

Patrick couldn't imagine it either. He was always bored of the beach after an hour. But, stung by Lou's implication that he didn't know how to relax and have a good time, he had asked Ariel the night before if she wanted to go away for a week. She had leapt at the idea, as he had known that she would. The Maldives had been her choice, and, as Patrick couldn't think of anywhere else he wanted to go, the Maldives it was.

'I have hidden shallows,' he told Lou, who was surprised into a laugh.

Patrick wished she wouldn't do that. It always startled him to see how vivid she looked when she laughed, how very different from the prim and proper PA he half wished she had remained.

'It's a long way to go for a week,' she warned. 'Why don't you make it a fortnight?'

Patrick thought about a week on a beach with Ariel's chatter. She was an extraordinarily pretty girl, but she did *talk*. 'A week will be quite long enough,' he said. 'You're only taking a week anyway.'

'Yes, but that's because Grace and Tom have to go back to school the following week,' she pointed out. 'And we're only going to the Yorkshire Dales, which is a bit different from a long-haul flight to the Maldives.'

He didn't want to remind her that he was only going on holiday because she was. It would sound a bit pathetic. 'Why Yorkshire?' he asked instead.

'My aunt lives there. My parents died when I was quite young, and since then Fenny has been the closest I've got to a mother. She lives in a lovely village, right in the Dales, and she's got the most beautiful garden. It's not quite the Indian Ocean,' she said, 'but it's always like going home for me. I'll be happy grubbing around in the garden and bullying the kids into long walks in the hills.'

And she had the nerve to imply that he wouldn't enjoy lying on a beach! 'Whatever turns you on,' he said, and then wished he'd chosen another phrase. Practically snatching the letters Lou was holding out to him, he headed towards his office before he could get distracted by wondering what else might turn her on.

It took Lou the best part of the morning to investigate hotels in the Maldives. She chose one whose prices made her eyes boggle, and then booked two first-class return flights, trying not to think about the train tickets she had bought with her family railcard the day before.

She had barely put down the phone to get on with some

of her own work when a quite distractingly beautiful girl drifted into her office. She had the kind of long, streaky blonde hair that looked as if she spent her life in the sun, and she constantly drew attention to it by shaking it away from her face.

As if that weren't bad enough, Lou noted sourly, she had glowing skin and enormous blue eyes and a perfect body, much of it visible given that she was only wearing a tiny skirt looped with a belt almost as big as it was, and a flimsy top that looked as if it consisted of a few scraps of material pinned together in a fit of absent-mindedness, but that probably cost a fortune.

Just being in the same room as her made Lou feel faded and grey and matronly.

'Can I help you?'

More shaking of the sun-streaked hair. 'Is Pat in?'

Pat? It took Lou a moment to work out whom she was talking about. *Pat?* Pat sounded far too warm and cuddly for Patrick. He wasn't a man who did warm and cuddly.

'I'm afraid he's in a meeting,' Lou said as pleasantly as she could.

'Oh.' The girl pouted, her beautiful mouth drooping. 'I need to talk to him about our holiday.'

'You must be Ariel,' said Lou. She had been dead right in her earlier speculations. Ariel could only be in her early twenties. Really, Patrick ought to be ashamed of himself. 'I've been booking the holiday for you this morning,' she told her.

Ariel's eyes flickered over her without interest. 'Oh, ya, Pat said he would ask his secretary to arrange it all.'

Oh, did he? Clearly she didn't even merit a name when he was talking to Ariel. Lou couldn't help feeling a little hurt.

'Well, don't worry, it's all arranged,' she said brightly.

Back went the hair again. 'I hope you've booked the Kandarai Beach Hotel?'

'No,' said Lou, keeping her voice determinedly even. 'I wasn't asked to book that. I've booked a really beautiful hotel on the grounds that it was the most luxurious one I could find.'

'Oh, but I wanted to go to the Kandarai Beach!' Ariel's beautiful face crumpled and for a moment she looked extraordinarily like Grace on the verge of a tantrum. 'That's what I wanted to talk to Pat about. I've been talking to my friend. She says it's *fabulous*. I didn't think you'd book it so quickly, but you can change it, can't you?'

'I can certainly mention it to Patrick,' said Lou. Frankly she had had enough of booking other people's luxury holidays in the Maldives for one morning.

'Mention what?' said Patrick's voice from the doorway. His eyes fell on Ariel, and he frowned, although Ariel didn't seem to notice his marked lack of delight at her unexpected appearance in his office.

'Oh, Pat, there you are!' she cried, wafting over to wind her arms around his neck and kiss him.

Patrick had little choice but to kiss her back, but as he lifted his head his eyes met Lou's, dark and ironic, over Ariel's blonde hair. He glared at her expression, but Lou just looked up at the ceiling, all innocence.

Annoyed, he put Ariel away from him. 'Ariel, what are you doing here? You know I don't like mixing work and pleasure.'

'Oh, *you*!' Ariel gave a girlish moue that made Lou cringe. 'I was just so excited about our holiday, I wanted to make sure that it was all perfect, and it's just as well I did,' she said. 'Pat, she's booked the wrong hotel!'

'You mean Lou,' said Patrick, frowning.

'Whatever.' Ariel waved Lou aside as unimportant. 'Oh,

Pat, please, please, *please* tell her to book the Kandarai Beach! I'll be so happy.' She was clinging girlishly to his arm, gazing up at him with her big blue eyes. 'I'll love you for ever!'

Oops, *big* mistake, Ariel, thought Lou, a reluctant witness to this simpering display. Even Ariel couldn't have missed the flash of irritation in Patrick's face.

He glanced at Lou in naked appeal. Clearly his only concern right then was to shut Ariel up and get her out of the office.

'I'll see what I can do,' she told him coolly and his features relaxed a bit.

Apparently Ariel had missed his look of irritation. Either that or she was monumentally thick-skinned. 'Ooh, thank you, thank you, thank you,' she said to Patrick, although he wasn't the one who was going to spend the afternoon on the phone. Ariel was wriggling with ecstasy. 'Let's go and have lunch and celebrate!'

'I haven't got time for lunch today,' said Patrick abruptly. 'I've got a meeting.'

Ariel shook more hair around so that it shone like spun gold in the light. 'I'll see you tonight, then,' she said, with a little pout.

Patrick evaded that neatly. 'I'll call you,' he said. 'Now, I'm sorry, Ariel, but I'm very busy.'

Lou didn't know whether she was glad to see Ariel go, or outraged at the passive way the girl accepted Patrick's brush-off. Ariel seemed perfectly happy, though, as well she might given that she was getting a free week in a luxury hotel in the Maldives.

At the door, she turned back with a final shake of her tresses and blew Patrick a kiss. 'Enjoy!' she said, and drifted off.

Patrick met Lou's eyes. 'Don't say a word,' he warned.

Lou preserved an innocent expression. 'I wouldn't dream of it,' she said, and picked up a file. 'Here are those figures you wanted.'

'Thank you.'

She couldn't resist it. 'You know, that would sound so much more sincere if you said it three times and promised to love me for ever,' she said sweetly, just as he reached his office door.

Patrick turned to glare at her, but Lou just laughed, and blew him a kiss in perfect imitation of Ariel. 'Enjoy!' she simpered and had the huge satisfaction of making Patrick stomp into his office and slam the door behind him.

She was less amused when Ariel took to calling every day, having evidently decided that Lou was her own private travel agent. After many phone calls and a lot of string-pulling, Lou had finally managed to book a suite at the Kandarai Beach Hotel, but this wasn't enough for Ariel. It turned out that she didn't want a suite, she wanted one of the luxuriously furnished huts that were built out over the water, so Lou had to rearrange it all again.

Then Ariel wanted to leave a day later so that she could go to some party, and as soon as Lou had done that she wanted her ticket changed again so that she could come back via Mombasa. A day later, she needed Lou to find out whether the hotel would be able to provide soya milk as she was allergic to dairy products.

By the time half-term came round, Lou's jaw was aching from keeping her teeth in a permanently gritted position. Ariel hadn't bothered to remember her name, but was constantly on the phone throwing her insubstantial weight around.

Hazel in Finance said that Ariel was a model. Lou wasn't surprised. Ariel certainly had the looks for it. She had the personality, too. Lou knew she was being unfair, and that there were probably loads of perfectly nice, pleasant models out there, but Ariel fulfilled every stereotype of a spoilt and manipulative prima donna, constantly demanding attention. Lou couldn't imagine what Patrick ever found to talk to her about.

But then, they probably didn't do a whole lot of talking, Lou realised, feeling depressed. It had been so long since she had slept with anyone, she could hardly remember what it was like. She was sure that she had forgotten how to do it. Most of the time she just accepted the absence of physical comfort as the price of refusing to get emotionally involved, and since she couldn't imagine sleeping with a man unless she loved him, and she wasn't going to risk the pain and heartbreak that accompanied love, it looked as if she might as well carry on accepting it.

She was better off sticking to gardening, Lou told herself. She might not be spending a week of passion and romance in the Indian Ocean, but she would have a week weeding instead, and very happy she would be with it.

It was a relief to leave Ariel and her ceaseless demands behind when they left for Yorkshire, but Lou couldn't help comparing her crowded train journey with Patrick's first-class flight. She cheered herself up by remembering that, although he might be surrounded by all the trappings of luxury, he would still have Ariel yakking non-stop beside him.

Then she looked across at Grace, slumped in the seat opposite, her mouth turned down sulkily, and Tom, riveted to his Game Boy, and she sighed to herself. Patrick probably wouldn't envy her her travelling companions either.

Fenny met them at the station in Skipton and drove them home. That tended to be a nerve-racking experience, as both the car and Fenny were getting on, and her aunt had only ever been an erratic driver at best, but as soon as Lou got out of the car and took a deep breath, savouring the clean, sharp air of the hills, she felt better. Even the children perked up. They might grumble and groan about being taken to the country, but they loved Fenny.

Yes, it had been a good idea to come here, Lou decided. She wasn't going to think about the bills waiting to be paid. She wasn't going to think about work. She wasn't going to think about anything.

Especially she wasn't going to think about Patrick.

But at odd times during the week Lou found her mind drifting to the Indian Ocean in spite of herself. She'd be pulling out weeds in Fenny's front garden, and suddenly she'd be wondering what Patrick was doing right then. Was he walking along a palm-fringed beach, hand in hand with Ariel? Were they frolicking in the minty green waters of a lagoon? Probably not, Lou decided on that one. She couldn't picture Patrick frolicking.

Or were they simply spending the entire week in bed?

'You seem very distracted at the moment, Lou,' said Fenny. She had brought out two cups of tea, and they sat companionably together on the doorstep as they drank them.

'I'm sorry, I didn't mean to be,' said Lou guiltily. 'I suppose I've just got things on my mind at the moment.'

'What kind of things?'

Patrick in bed, his body bare and brown against white sheets...

'Oh, you know...the usual things. Bills to pay, new shoes to buy for the kids.' She smiled, but it didn't quite work. 'It would help if they would stop growing!'

'I thought it might be a man,' said Fenny casually.

Since when had her aunt been telepathic? Lou attempted a laugh. 'Oh, Fenny, I'm too old for all that now!'

'Nonsense!' Fenny sounded quite cross. 'You're never

too old for *all that*!' She sighed. 'I keep hoping that you'll tell me you're getting married again,' she admitted. 'It would be such a shame if that Lawrence put you off men altogether. They're not all low-down, irresponsible cheats, you know.'

Fenny had never liked Lawrie and the feeling had been mutual. 'It would just be so much *easier* for you if you had a husband. Someone to help you. It's very hard for you to deal with everything on your own.'

Lou couldn't help thinking about the fantasy she had confessed to Patrick. 'It sounds good, Fenny,' she said lightly, 'but it's not that easy to find men who want to do that.'

'I know.' Fenny shot her a speculative sideways glance. 'I just wondered if you had met someone likely already. There's something different about you,' she said thoughtfully.

For some reason, Lou's mind flashed to Patrick, and a tiny blush crept up her cheeks. 'No, there's no one.'

No one the slightest bit likely, anyway.

She had herself well back under control by the time she got into work the following Monday, though. She was standing in front of her desk, glancing through the pile of messages, when Patrick strode in, and although her heart did its usual little lurch Lou was proud of the cool way she could smile at him.

'Hello,' she said, quite as if she hadn't spent most of the previous week imagining him stretched out in bed, his body lean and brown, a lazy grin on his face.

Patrick stopped at the sight of her, neat and dark and as immaculately turned out as ever. She was wearing a straight grey skirt and pale pink shirt, with just a glimpse of pearls at her neck. Not an exciting outfit, but after a week of women in bikinis, or shorts and skimpy dresses, Lou looked cool and classy.

'Oh,' he said. 'It's you.'

Lou lifted her brows. 'It *is* my office,' she pointed out. 'It shouldn't be that big a surprise to find me here.'

'I didn't think you'd be in yet,' Patrick said, hating the way she could make him feel like a fool sometimes.

'I wasn't expecting you either.' No one knew his flight times better than Lou, who had had to change them so often. He wouldn't have got back until late the night before. 'Did you have a good holiday?'

'No,' said Patrick, and went into his office, shutting the door with a snap.

'I had a lovely week too, thanks,' said Lou to the closed door. 'Nice of you to ask!'

At his desk, Patrick switched on his computer with a scowl. It had been a long week and he was glad to be back in the office and away from Ariel, who had taken the invitation to spend a holiday together as a sign of irreversible commitment on his part. Alternately possessive and coyly flirtatious, she had simply ignored his increasingly blunt attempts to explain that, as far as he was concerned, there was no question of a long-term relationship, let alone marriage.

Patrick cursed himself for ever asking her. He had only done it to prove something to Lou, and it didn't help that he couldn't now remember what that something was. All he knew was that it was somehow Lou's fault.

In the evenings he had sat and watched the sun set over the Indian Ocean in a spectacular blaze of colour, and inexplicably his mind had drifted to the Yorkshire Dales. As the hot wind had soughed through the palm trees, Patrick had found himself thinking about clean, fresh air and green hills. He had imagined Lou, sitting and talking in a fragrant garden as the light faded in the long, unspectacular English summer twilight, and he had been alarmed at how appealing it had all seemed.

There was something wrong with him, Patrick had decided irritably. There he was, on a beautiful tropical island, in unimaginable luxury, unobtrusive staff on hand to gratify his every whim. With him was a girl who made every other man on the island look at him enviously. Ariel was gorgeous, there were no two ways about it. Beautiful, sexy, with glowing skin, a fantastic body and legs up to her armpits, she was every man's fantasy come true.

So why was he sitting there thinking about a middle-aged woman with lines starring her eyes? Lou had good legs, but she was hardly the stuff of fantasy, was she? It was just that Patrick had found himself longing for a dose of her cool irony in place of Ariel's inane chatter, for her crisp retorts, for the gleam of humour in her dark gaze, and the direct way she looked into his eyes instead of coyly sweeping down her lashes and peeping from beneath them the way Ariel did.

And then he had found himself remembering how warm and vivid Lou had seemed that night in Newcastle, how she had let down that barrier of poise and let him glimpse the sensuous woman beneath, and he had found himself wishing, too, that he could see her that way again.

He had thought about what she had suggested that night, too. He had thought about it a lot.

Patrick threw himself down in his chair and swung it round in exasperation. He hated feeling like this, edgy and uncertain about everything. He wasn't himself.

Look at the way he had behaved just now. He'd been thinking about Lou, and when he'd walked into the office and found her there his heart had leapt ridiculously. She had smiled, but it had only been her polite smile, and then she had lifted her brows and he had felt an idiot. Clearly she wasn't overjoyed to see him, the way he was to see her, and Patrick had been so disappointed that he had just grunted and slammed into his office.

He would have to apologise. If only she didn't make him feel so unsettled. Patrick drummed his fingers on the desk, wondering how to word what he wanted to say.

'I'm sorry I was a bit abrupt earlier,' he said when she had come into his office and they had been through the urgent business.

'That's all right,' said Lou. 'I'm sorry you didn't have a good time. Was there a problem with the hotel?'

'No.'

'Did you have good weather?'

'Perfect, and, before you ask, the flights were on time and all your arrangements worked precisely.' He hesitated. 'How was your holiday?'

'Well, the trains were late and the weather was awful, but it was beautiful and Fenny's a great cook, so it was a very relaxing break. Just what I needed.'

'Good,' said Patrick, but he knew that he sounded grouchy. Obviously she hadn't missed *him* at all. She'd been quite happy having a good time with her children and aunt.

That seemed to be the end of the holiday interrogation. It didn't look as if there would be a friendly exchange of holiday snaps when the photos were developed. Lou gathered up her notebook and pen and rose from her seat.

'Don't go,' said Patrick brusquely. 'I want to talk to you.'

Subsiding back into her chair, Lou opened her notebook once more and held her pen at the ready.

'You won't need to take notes,' he said, disconcerted by her businesslike demeanour.

He was doing this all wrong, he realised. He should have waited until the evening and taken her out for a drink, but it was too late for that now. He shrugged mentally. He might as well deal with it now that he'd got this far.

'This is personal,' he explained.

'Oh?'

Lou laid down her pen and regarded him with a certain wariness.

Having got this far, Patrick wasn't sure how to proceed. He got to his feet and prowled around the office, his hands thrust into his pockets and his brows drawn together.

'I've been thinking about what you said,' he said at last, coming to a halt by the window.

'What *I* said? When?'

'That night in Newcastle.' He turned to look at her.

Tell-tale colour crept into Lou's cheeks. Trust Patrick to bring that up now, just when she had allowed herself to relax and think that the whole sorry incident was forgotten.

'I shouldn't pay any attention to anything I said that night.' She tried to make a joke of it. 'I'd had far too much champagne.'

'You said I should think about marrying you,' said Patrick. 'And that's what I've been doing. I think you were right. I think we should get married.'

CHAPTER FIVE

LOU stared at him. 'I wasn't being serious!'

'I know, but the more I think about it, the more sensible it seems.'

Sensible...? 'Hang on,' said Lou. 'Is this a joke?'

'If you'd had the week I've just had, you'd know I'm not in a joking mood,' said Patrick. 'It was a mistake taking Ariel on holiday, I can see that now. She took it to mean that I was ready for commitment. And you didn't tell me that the Maldives were full of honeymooners,' he added accusingly.

'I'm not responsible for you knowing what anyone who's ever picked up a holiday brochure knows,' said Lou at her most crisp.

Patrick glowered. 'It was a disaster. Ariel spent her entire time angling for an engagement ring. I told her that it wasn't going to happen, but that didn't stop her giggling about weddings with new brides and picking up tips about dresses and table decorations and what the best man ought to wear,' he said with distaste.

'I came home vowing that I was never going to get in that situation again. I've decided that the only way to convince girls that a relationship with me doesn't involve any measure of commitment is to show them I'm already married.'

Lou could hardly believe what she was hearing. 'You don't think that's taking your fantasy about sex without a relationship a bit far?' she asked acidly.

'Why? It would make the point, wouldn't it?'

She shook her head in disbelief. 'Why would you want to get involved with a woman who was prepared to sleep with a married man?'

'But that's the whole point,' said Patrick impatiently. 'I don't want to be involved. I'm not interested in anything beyond a purely physical relationship. I always make that clear anyway, but maybe they would believe me if they knew I had a wife in the background.'

'There is such a thing as divorce, you know,' said Lou, exasperated. 'What's to stop these poor deluded girls hoping that you'll fall in love with them and leave your wife?'

Patrick thought for a moment. 'I'll tell them that I've signed a pre-nuptial contract so my wife gets seventy per cent of my assets if there's a divorce.'

Lou goggled at him. 'It might even be worth marrying you for that!' she said, still half convinced that he was joking.

'I'm serious,' said Patrick. He came back to sit opposite her and folded his hands on the desk. 'I'm offering you the chance of a life where you never have to worry about money again. All I ask in return is that you be a visible wife, that you'll help with corporate entertaining and play the convincing part of a wife in front of my business associates—and my mother and sisters,' he added as an afterthought.

'It's true that you're not absolutely ideal,' he went on, apparently unaware of Lou's expression of growing outrage. 'You're certainly not the kind of wife I ever envisaged for myself,' he admitted, 'and it's a pity that you've got children. I don't see myself as a stepfather, but I expect that we could work something out.'

There was always boarding-school, he thought to himself.

'I don't see why we'd need to have that much to do with

each other,' said Patrick, dismissing that objection. 'So while you're not exactly what I want, you have got other advantages to offset that, especially your knowledge of the business, as you pointed out yourself. And being older means that you're mature enough to understand that marriage would be a purely practical arrangement on both sides. And, of course, you've got more of an incentive than most,' he finished. 'You need the money.'

'Not that much,' said Lou distinctly. Now she knew how Elizabeth Bennett had felt when Mr Darcy had insulted her family and her connections and then tossed a proposal of marriage her way.

She got to her feet.

'Where are you going?' asked Patrick, taken aback.

'Back to work.'

'But what about my proposal?'

'Oh, that was a *proposal*, was it?' said Lou in her most sarcastic voice. 'I didn't realise an answer was required.'

'Of course I want an answer,' said Patrick crossly. What did she think, he was just having a chat?

'Oh, OK.' Lou put her head on one side and pretended to think about it for an insultingly short time. 'No.'

'No?' He was outraged.

'No,' she repeated firmly. 'As proposals go, that one sucked! There's absolutely no question of me marrying you, Patrick. You'd better find someone else to solve your commitment problem, because it's certainly not going to be me!'

Patrick got to his feet too. 'Just a minute, this was *your* idea,' he said angrily.

'I can't believe you took me seriously,' said Lou, just as angry. Angrier, in fact, and getting more and more angry the more she thought about it. 'I'd been guzzling champagne all evening, for heaven's sake! Of *course* I wasn't serious!'

'You were pretty persuasive!'

'I certainly wouldn't have been if I'd known you were going to take a joke and use it to insult me!'

'I've just asked you to marry me,' said Patrick, livid by now. 'How is that insulting you?'

'What kind of woman do you think I am?' she demanded furiously. 'Do you really think I'd marry a man I don't love, a man I don't even *like* very much, just for his money? A man who tells me outright that he can't be bothered with my children, a man who doesn't really want me at all or find me that attractive, but thinks I'll do and that I'm desperate enough to agree?

'I've got to tell you, Patrick, that I find that pretty insulting,' she told him. 'I mean, I've heard of some insensitive proposals in my time, but yours has to take the biscuit!'

'What was I supposed to do, go down on one knee and wrap it up in a lot of romantic claptrap? Don't tell me you expected me to tell you I loved you?'

Lou drew in a sharp breath. 'I *expected* you to treat me with some respect,' she said in an arctic accent.

'I was being honest!' he protested.

'Oh, yes, you were honest, all right. You made your position crystal-clear. You think you can buy me the way you can buy all the other women in your life. Well, I may not have a lot of money, but I'm not for sale!'

Patrick struggled to control his temper, not very successfully. 'Listen, it was you who were so full of what a perfect wife you'd be and what a good thing it would be for you if you married me. It would be your fantasy, you said.'

'I can assure you that a proposal like that has *never* figured in a fantasy of mine,' said Lou, her voice still glacial. 'I've already been told by one husband that I'm not really the kind of wife he wanted,' she added bitterly. 'I can do without another husband thinking the same thing. And if you think I'm going to expose my children to the kind of attitude that treats young women as objects, and women over forty as past their sell-by date, you've got another think coming!

'Your mother's right,' she swept on, too consumed by hurt and anger to care about her job any more. 'You *are* selfish. You think that because you're rich, you can have whatever you want, and never have to give anything in return. Well, I'm sorry, but that's not a lesson I want Grace and Tom to learn. They've got few enough role models as it is, and I'm certainly not going to provide them with one of such monumental selfishness!'

'I never suggested not giving you anything in return,' Patrick ground out. 'I was proposing to give you quite a lot of money, if you remember.'

'I'm not talking about money,' said Lou contemptuously. 'I'm talking about feelings.'

'Oh, *feelings*!' he sneered.

'Yes, those things you don't have and the rest of us do. You go on and on about how your girlfriends hassle you about commitment, but have you ever thought what it's like for them to be with you and get their emotions thrown back in their faces all the time?'

'Listen, nobody's forcing them. If they don't want to go out with me, they can say no.'

'Yes, well, I'm saying no too,' said Lou. 'I want my children to believe that it's possible for adults to live together in a loving relationship. They're not stupid. They're not likely to find that very convincing if they saw you carrying on with your…*floozies*…and treating me as a housekeeper, only coming home whenever it suits you.'

Patrick raked his hands through his hair in frustration. 'You might want to think some time about exposing your children to the realities of life,' he bit out. 'All those romantic ideals aren't going to be much use to them when they get out into the big, bad world and realise that nothing is free. If you want anything, you have to work for it, one way or another. Why should marriage be any different?'

'Because unless it *is* different, there's no point in getting married!' Lou exploded. 'It shouldn't be about who gets what, it should be about sharing.'

Tears of sheer anger, and more than a little hurt, were perilously close. She turned for the door. 'I'm sorry if I gave you the wrong impression in Newcastle. I had hoped that you would be able to forget that conversation. I'll certainly try to forget this one,' she said in a freezing voice.

'If that's what you want,' said Patrick, equally icy.

'I'll let you have these letters to sign as soon as I've done them,' said Lou coolly and went out, closing the door carefully behind her.

As soon as she had gone, Patrick vented his feelings on his chair, something that hurt him a lot more than the chair. He couldn't believe that she had said no and walked out like that. Not once had he considered that she would turn him down. He was Patrick Farr and he always got what he wanted.

Until now.

He raged silently as he hopped around, nursing his sore foot. How dared Lou talk to him like that? He had offered her a solution to all her problems, and he would have been generous. Did she have any idea what she was giving up?

Well, if she didn't want to marry him, that was fine, he told himself. It was probably a good thing. He could have done without the last few humiliating minutes, but he'd be perfectly happy to carry on his life as before. *He* wasn't the one who had lost the chance to change his life. Oh, no, he wasn't going to be the one with the regrets.

'Mum, I need a new pair of trainers,' Tom greeted Lou when she picked him up that night.

Lou's heart sank. Tom was growing so fast. He seemed to need a new pair of trainers every few months, and they were always so expensive. They had to be the right brand and the right style and the right colour. In her day they had just had plimsolls. Whatever had happened to them?

'We'll get you some this weekend,' she promised.

'Cool. Can we go into town to where Charlie got his?'

Charlie was Tom's best friend and rival in everything. He was a nice boy, but Lou sometimes wished his parents didn't indulge him quite so much. But then she would feel guilty about being unfair. If she could afford it, she would probably want to do the same for Tom as Charlie's parents did for him.

'Charlie's going to a brilliant sports course in the summer,' Tom told her, hoisting his backpack onto his thin shoulders. 'You go off to this place for two weeks and they give you special coaching and you get to try a lot of new sports as well. Can I go?'

Lou looked down at his eager face and her heart twisted. The only thing Tom loved more than sport was cars, and fortunately he was still too young to indulge that particular taste. He would get so much out of a sports course like that, but it was bound to be expensive.

'We'll see, Tom,' she said and his face fell.

'It's not fair,' he said, scuffing his shoes along the pavement. 'Whenever you say, "We'll see", it means no. I'm just as good at football as Charlie, but he'll get extra coaching and I'll be left behind. I probably won't even get in the team next year,' he said bitterly.

There was worse to come when Grace danced in. She had always been a volatile child, changing moods with bewildering speed. When she was happy, she was wonderful company, but she could just as easily make life a misery for everyone in the vicinity. The latter had been her preferred option since turning teenager with a vengeance, although there were still moments when Lou recognised the enchanting child she had been when she was small.

'Mum, look!' she said breathlessly, waving a piece of paper around. 'There's going to be a skiing trip to the Rockies next year. *Please* say I can go!'

'Skiing?' Tom's face lit up. 'Can I go? I want to try snowboarding.'

'It's not for your year, squirt,' said Grace, whipping the paper out of his reach. 'What do you think, Mum?' she added anxiously. 'Can I go?'

Lou's head was aching with tension after that row with Patrick, and she had come home to find three bills and an ominously worded letter from her bank suggesting that she make an appointment to see her personal manager.

'Can I see what it says?'

Grace relinquished the piece of paper reluctantly. She was too excited to sit still and kept jumping up and down from the kitchen table. 'Emily went last year, and she was, like, it was so excellent. They stayed in this log-cabin-type place and went out every night and the snow was this high.' She gestured up to her shoulder for Tom's benefit.

Lou listened to her chattering on, and tried to concentrate on the details the school had sent out. She fastened at last on the cost of the trip. As suspected, she couldn't even afford the deposit as things stood at the moment.

She bit her lip. Grace was so excited, she couldn't bear

to disappoint her. And Tom deserved a chance at that course. She would have to see if Lawrie could help. He might be going through a flush period. You could never tell with Lawrie.

'Let me talk to your father,' she said.

'Oh, Mum, he won't do anything,' wailed Grace. 'He said he was going to take us to Greece this summer, but then he went and bought that stupid sports car, and now he says he can't afford to go anywhere.'

'It's a cool car,' said Tom loyally. 'It's an Audi Quattro coupé. He's got a personalised number plate too.'

Lou wanted to scream. A sports car! Why could Lawrie never think of his children first? Oh, there would be some plausible excuse. He would explain very patiently that he needed the car to project the right image for his new company, a company that would no doubt go the way of all the others Lawrie had lost interest in.

'Mum, Dad won't help,' said Grace bitterly. 'He never does. He'll say that he will, and then he won't.'

That just about summed Lawrie up.

Lou hated the look on her daughter's face. There wasn't anything she could do now about Lawrie's relationship with his children, but she wished he understood how much he hurt them whenever he let them down. Grace and Tom loved their father, but they had learnt not to rely on him.

Lou knew what that felt like.

She sighed. 'I'll see what I can do,' was all she could promise Grace, who slumped down at the kitchen table, her excitement evaporated.

Lawrie wasn't a bad man. He wasn't malicious or deliberately hurtful. He was intelligent and funny, and charm itself when it suited him, but he was also thoughtless and utterly self-centred. Lou didn't mind for herself any more, but she did mind for the children. It wasn't the life she had wanted to give them. She had tried so hard for so long to shield them from the consequences of their father's feckless attitude to life, but the reality was that Lawrie had chosen to leave them. He had chosen a new family, and there was nothing she could do to make that better for them.

They had lost their father and their home, and it hadn't been easy for either of them. Lou was doing her best. She loved them unconditionally, she comforted them when they were upset, she fed them and cared for them and encouraged them, and gave them the security and stability they didn't know they needed. She had been careful never to talk bitterly about Lawrie in front of them, great as the temptation was at times. It was Lou who rang him to remind him when their birthdays were, who suggested ways he could meet up with Grace and Tom, and who made sure they rang him regularly.

And she tried to give them as much fun as she could, although she was bitterly aware that a lot of the time she was too worn down by work and worry to give them as much of that as they needed. Lawrie was always good at fun, but Lawrie wasn't always there.

Lou ached for them sometimes. At times like now, knowing that she was going to end up disappointing them both, she would do anything to make things different for them.

About to lay aside the note Grace had given her, Lou stopped with her hand outstretched.

Anything?

Including marrying Patrick Farr?

She looked down at the note once more. Where else could she possibly find the extra money she'd need to send Grace on this holiday? And if Grace went skiing, Tom could go on his sports course…

At the kitchen table, Grace was slumped in a familiar posture, leaning on one arm, her dark curly hair hanging over her face. Lou could just see the tip of her nose as she traced despondent patterns on the tabletop with one finger. Opposite her, Tom had dropped his backpack on the floor and was crouched over it, tossing pens, bits of paper and chocolate wrappers carelessly aside as he rummaged through it. Probably *not* looking for his homework, judging by his enthusiasm.

As she watched them Lou felt the familiar clutch of love so intense it was almost painful. It was easy to say, 'I'd do anything for my kids', but was she prepared to do it?

Thoughtfully, she opened the fridge and took out some tomatoes. Pasta again tonight. It was cheap, cheerful and nutritious, but sometimes she got so sick of cooking it. She picked her way through Tom's discarded mess and removed the ironing basket so that she could get into the cupboard and find some oil. That was another thing about this flat. There was no room to put anything.

If she married Patrick, there would be plenty of room for them all to spread themselves. She thought about his six bedrooms. Perhaps if they weren't living on top of each other the way they were now, they wouldn't be so irritable with each other.

Outside, it was a beautiful summer evening, but it was hard to tell from in here, overshadowed as they were by the backs of the house behind them. The backyards in this area were dark and gloomy at the best of times, but at least if you had one you could step outside and look up at the sky.

Patrick probably had a garden, mused Lou. She could grow fresh herbs, and when she was making pasta like this she could go out and pick some basil, some oregano, maybe, or some parsley. She could stand with the herbs in her hand and smell the grass and feel the sun on her face.

All she had to do was marry Patrick.

* * *

Lou moistened her lips nervously. 'Could I have a word with you?'

Patrick had been in meetings most of the day, which was a relief in one way. The atmosphere that morning had been inevitably arctic, but Lou was desperate not to lose her nerve. Having made her decision, she hadn't got a chance to even raise the matter until Patrick had come back at five o'clock, which meant that she had spent the entire day dithering about what to say.

Daunted by his air of chilly reserve, Lou gave him his messages and made her request. It was now or never. She couldn't spend another night like the last one, tossing and turning in an agony of indecision.

Patrick looked at her properly for the first time that day, his eyes a glacial green. 'A word?'

'Well, a few words.' Lou took a deep breath. 'I…I wanted to apologise for the way I reacted yesterday,' she said. 'You made a fair offer. I just…wasn't expecting it, and I overreacted. I'm sorry.'

Something shifted in Patrick's expression. 'I'm the one who should be apologising to you,' he said gruffly. 'I didn't express myself well. When I thought about it afterwards, I wasn't surprised you were angry. So I'm sorry too.'

'The thing is…' Lou stopped, not sure how to ask if the offer was still open. She couldn't really blame Patrick if he had changed his mind after the fuss she had made.

'Look, why don't we start again?' said Patrick, coming to her rescue. 'But let's go somewhere we can talk properly, away from the office.' He looked at his watch. 'Do you have to go and pick up the children, or can you come and have a drink?'

Grace was going to do her homework with a friend, and Tom had football. 'A drink would be nice,' said Lou gratefully. She had a feeling she was going to need it.

Patrick glanced quickly through his messages. 'All of this can wait till tomorrow. Let's go now.'

Lou was very aware of him as they caught the lift down to the ground floor. He seemed guarded, which was fair enough after the way she'd spoken to him yesterday, but not as angry as she had expected. She wasn't sure what she was going to say. It seemed a colossal cheek to ask him to marry her after all—and without the benefit of a bucketload of champagne either.

Patrick took her to a quiet pub not far from the river. To Lou's delight it had a garden hidden away behind, with a couple of trees and some shrubs, and a few jolly geraniums in pots. They had beaten the rush-hour exodus and there was still a table.

'You sit there and make sure no one else gets it,' said Patrick, overbearing Lou's attempts to buy the drinks.

Closing her eyes and tipping her face to the sun, Lou felt some of the tension begin to seep out of her. It felt good to be outside, even in a crowded pub garden with the traffic roaring away at the front of the building. Of course, it would feel even better if she didn't have to ask her boss to marry her when he came back from the bar.

'Here you go.' Her eyes snapped open as Patrick set the drinks down on the table and sat opposite her on the bench. He had left his jacket in the office and was in shirtsleeves, rolled up to his wrists.

The sight of him was giving Lou curious flutters inside, and it was difficult to know whether they were caused by nerves or a much more primitive attraction. Either way, they had left her in the grip of a paralysing shyness, and she sipped her gin and tonic nervously, trying desperately to think of a way to start.

She couldn't do it. There was no way she could calmly

ask Patrick if she could change her mind about marrying him, after everything she had had to say yesterday about not being the kind of woman who would marry for money. No way. She must have been mad to have even considered it.

She would pretend she wanted to talk about her overtime, Lou decided.

But then she remembered Grace's face, lit up with excitement at the thought of a skiing holiday, of going somewhere different and doing something different and meeting different people. And she remembered the way Tom's shoulders had slumped when she had said, 'We'll see.'

She thought about the cramped flat where sometimes it felt hard to breathe, and where the neighbours conducted their arguments at the tops of their voices so that Grace and Tom knew more than they ought to about the most intimate details of married life.

And then she thought about being married to Patrick and her insides squirmed and fluttered and generally made it impossible to get to grips with anything else.

The silence stretched uncomfortably. Lou's eyes wandered desperately around the garden, but she was very conscious of Patrick sitting opposite her. With his shirtsleeves rolled up, she could see his forearms, browner than usual after a week in the Maldives, and her gaze kept snagging on the fine hairs at his wrist and the strong, square hands playing with his glass.

Patrick was nervous too, she realised slowly. It gave her the confidence to launch into speech.

'I've been thinking—'

She began just as Patrick said, 'I probably shouldn't say this, but—'

They both stopped, feeling foolish.

'You first,' he said awkwardly.

Lou squared her shoulders and took a breath. Just do it. 'Look, you were honest with me yesterday, so I might as well be the same today. I was furious when you made that proposal, but I thought about it a lot last night and I was wondering...well, if it was too late to change my mind.'

There, it was done.

Patrick had spent the previous night trying to convince himself that he had had a lucky escape. The whole idea had been ridiculous, and if he hadn't had such an awful holiday he would probably never have considered it. What if Lou had accepted him? He would have been saddled with two adolescent stepchildren and a middle-aged wife. Madness.

So the rush of relief he felt at her words didn't make much sense. He was still raw with hurt and humiliation at her flat rejection—*a man I don't even like*, she had told him—mingled with guilt at the botched way he had handled things. He had hurt Lou, too, and it wasn't a nice feeling.

He drank his beer carefully. 'What made you change your mind?'

'Money,' said Lou bleakly. She told him about the skiing trip and Tom's sports course. 'I'm tired of struggling and disappointing the kids. Yesterday you offered me a chance to change that.'

She hesitated. 'I know I had a lot to say about not being the kind of person who married for money, but maybe I am that person. Maybe I have to be. I've tried marrying for love, and that didn't work out, so this time perhaps I should think about marrying for a different reason, for my children. That may be the right thing to do.'

'You don't sound that convinced,' commented Patrick, his eyes still guarded.

'I'm not entirely convinced,' Lou admitted. 'That's really

what I wanted to talk to you about. I wanted to ask you if I could think about it a bit. I can't decide anything until Grace and Tom have met you, and you've met them.' She managed a feeble smile. 'You might change *your* mind then!'

Patrick's expression was unreadable, but at least he wasn't shouting at her or carrying on the way she had carried on when he had made *his* proposal. Lou ploughed on.

'I was wondering if we could keep our options open,' she said. 'Perhaps we could have lunch or something together, and then see if we think it could still work?' She swallowed. 'We might decide to forget the whole idea, or we might decide it could work after all, in which case we could talk about what we would both expect out of a marriage like that.'

'That makes sense,' said Patrick. A lot more sense than springing the idea on her, tossing down a proposal and demanding an immediate answer. It was what he should have suggested in the first place. 'All right, let's do it that way.'

For the first time a smile touched the corners of his mouth. 'What are you doing this weekend? Why don't you bring them to lunch on Sunday? It would give you all a chance to see where you could be living if nothing else.' He hesitated. 'I've got to say that I've got no experience of entertaining children of that age, but there's a pool if they like swimming. They just need to bring their things.'

By Sunday, Lou had talked herself in and out of the idea so many times that she didn't know *what* she thought any more. But it was too late to back out of lunch, so they would all go. She had this idea that if she could just see Patrick with the children, she would know what to do.

It was hard to imagine them getting on, though. Patrick

had no interest in children, and Grace and Tom would make it very clear if they didn't like him. Lou foresaw a disastrous lunch.

Well, if it was a disaster, her decision would be made, she decided resolutely. She would just tell Patrick that marriage wouldn't work, and she would find some other way to send Grace skiing. And Tom would get his sports course as well.

She would do it. Somehow.

But she would try Patrick's option first.

CHAPTER SIX

PATRICK lived in a quiet street in Chelsea that positively smelled of money. Lou felt as if, somewhere between there and the tube, they had wandered into a parallel universe that had no relation whatsoever to the busy road in Tooting where they lived. She had known Patrick was wealthy, of course, but this was the first time she had come face to face with the reality of how different his life was from hers.

It felt very uncomfortable. This was a street peopled by different beings and the three of them didn't belong here. It had been a mistake to come.

Lou had done her best to make the children presentable, but she wasn't sure that Patrick would appreciate the chains looped around Grace's waist or her enormous clumpy boots. Her curly hair, inherited from her father, was a mess. Lou's fingers itched for a comb, but Grace had absolutely refused to brush it. She was going through a Goth phase, and she considered that she had made enough concessions by not wearing black lipstick.

Tom was less trendy, but no more neat. Lou was resigned to that by now. He was one of those boys that you could send out of the door looking well scrubbed and immaculate, and by the time he was at the end of the street his hair would be sticking up in tufts, his top would have parted company with his trousers and his shoelaces would be undone.

Today he was wearing scruffy trainers, saggy jeans and a T-shirt that had been clean when they'd left the house, but which had mysteriously acquired a dirty mark somewhere along the line, probably when he'd been messing around on the underground escalators.

Only the promise of a swim in a private pool had resigned the children to a boring lunch, but they were clearly impressed by the wealth that practically oozed out of the front doors of these houses. There were no terraced houses here. No flats, no shops, no take-aways or minicab firms. Each house stood in its own grounds, partially hidden by high hedges, so that you just caught the odd glimpse of the luxury within through the gates.

Tom's steps slowed down as they passed each entrance, straining to get a look at the cars parked on the crisp gravel. 'Wow, look at that!' he said, offering a running commentary of the vehicles on display as he craned his neck to see through the gates. 'BMW...Mercedes...Mercedes...Rolls Royce...Porsche...Jaguar...'

'Your boss must be rolling in it if he lives here,' said Grace.

Lou didn't answer. She felt slightly sick, and her nerve was rapidly deserting her. It was all very well wanting financial security, but this kind of wealth was just obscene. She couldn't possibly marry Patrick. It would never work. She was much too old to play Cinderella.

'Is this it?' Grace had stopped and was staring at a house set back from the road, her voiced awed.

Lou dug out the address and checked the number. 'Thirty-three...yes, it looks like this is it.' She swallowed as she looked at the house. 'Gosh.'

Joining her daughter at the iron gates, she peered through at a large, handsome house with large windows, its cream stucco front softened by a wonderful climbing hydrangea. A sweep of gravel led up to the imposing front door, and the front garden had been cleverly planted to keep the house as private as possible without overshadowing it.

Tom trailed up and the three of them stood there looking at it, their hands on the railings of the gate, like prisoners staring longingly at the outside world.

'Mum…' Tom drew a deep breath of wonderment. 'Mum, is that his car?'

Lou hadn't even noticed the car sitting in front of the house. 'Er…maybe. I don't know,' she said nervously.

'How do we get in?' said Grace more practically.

There was an intercom on the massive gate post. Lou pressed the button, half expecting some venerable butler to answer. Or more likely a beefy security guard complete with snarling Rottweiler. But it was Patrick's voice that emerged from the speaker, crisp and unmistakable.

'It's me,' she said weakly. 'Lou. We're here.'

'Good,' he said. 'Come on in.'

The great gates swung open, and they slipped through, unnerved by how quickly the gates began to close behind them. 'It's like being in a prison,' whispered Grace as they headed towards the front door, their shoes crunching on the gravel, the sound unnaturally loud in the silence.

Ahead of them, the front door opened and suddenly Patrick was there, wearing chinos and a blue shirt open at the collar, but looking as formidable as ever in spite of his casual clothes.

For some reason, Lou was finding it hard to breathe properly. 'Hi,' she said in a stupid high voice, and felt Grace flick a surprised glance in her direction.

'Hello. Glad you could make it.' To her annoyance Patrick sounded exactly the same as usual. Shouldn't he be nervous too at the prospect of meeting her children? He might have seemed a little bit more effusive, or looked as if he was trying too hard. But no. He was just the way he always was, faintly brusque and to the point.

Clearing her throat, Lou put an arm round Grace. 'This is my daughter, Grace.'

Patrick and Grace sized each other up. At first all Patrick saw was a young girl with messy hair, dressed alarmingly in Goth gear, but when he looked closer he could see that she had an enchantingly pretty face, a very stubborn chin, and her mother's dark, direct eyes.

For her part, Grace saw a tall man in boring, conventional clothes, but she couldn't dismiss him the way she really wanted to. There was something uncompromising about him, a coolness to his eyes and a set to his mouth that indicated that he wasn't someone to mess with. Also, he wasn't trying to impress her, which she liked.

'Hello, Grace,' he said.

'Hi,' she said warily.

Lou let out a breath she hadn't realised she'd been holding. It might not sound like much of an exchange, but Grace was liable to take violent dislike to people on sight, often on the flimsiest of grounds—I didn't like his shoes, I didn't like the way she smiled at me, that sniff really annoyed me.

'And this—'

She stopped, realising for the first time that Tom wasn't by her side. Turning, she saw to her horror that her son had gravitated towards the car and had his nose squashed up against the driver's window, grubby hands pressed into the immaculate paintwork, oblivious to the greetings taking place at the door.

'Tom!' she said, aghast. 'What do you think you're doing? Come here at once.'

Tom didn't even turn round. 'Mum, do you know what this is?' he said reverently. 'It's a *Porsche 911*! Twin turbo!'

'I dare say,' said Lou, a distinct edge to her voice now. 'But leave it now and come and meet Patrick. *Now*, Tom.'

Tom glanced over his shoulder at that. 'But, Mum, you don't understand! This is *the best car in the world*!'

Lou looked helplessly at Patrick. 'I'm terribly sorry. He loves cars.'

'I can see.' Patrick went over to join Tom at the Porsche, surprised but pleased to discover a kindred spirit at last, even in the unlikely form of Lou's eleven-year-old son. He loved that car, but he never seemed to meet anyone else who understood how beautiful it was.

Women just didn't get it. They might like the idea of a sports car, but in Patrick's experience they didn't have a clue what made it really special. He had given up talking to them about cars. He was pretty sure, for instance, that if he asked Lou what kind of car she liked she would reply something annoying like 'one that goes' or 'a red one' as his sisters did.

'You're right,' he said to Tom. 'It *is* the best car in the world. Do you want to get in the driver's seat?'

Tom's eyes shone. 'Could I?' he breathed.

Patrick fished his key out of his pocket and pressed a button that sent the soft top sliding smoothly back as Tom opened the driver's door with the kind of awe usually reserved for cathedrals. Delighted at the chance to show off his car to someone who would really appreciate it, Patrick got in beside him, and soon the two heads were bent together over the dashboard.

Lou and Grace stood on the front steps, and listened as snatches of animated conversation about spoilers and revs per minute and six-speed manual gearboxes floated across the gravel.

Lou looked at Grace and Grace looked at Lou.

'We'll never get lunch now,' sighed Grace. 'You know what Tom's like.'

Lou went over to the car. 'We'll go in and make ourselves at home, shall we?' she suggested pleasantly.

The startled pause that followed made it pretty clear that Patrick had forgotten all about the two of them left stranded on the steps.

'Oh, yes, yes…do you mind?' he said, wrenching his attention from the dashboard with an effort. 'I'll just show Tom the engine. We'll just be a minute…'

It was clearly going to be a very long minute. Lou and Grace left them to it. Inside, there was a vast hall with a grand staircase leading up to a landing, and doors opening off it. Lou was dying to explore, but she didn't want to seem too nosy, so they followed the light through to the back of the house where an enormous, elegant conservatory housed a gleaming turquoise pool.

'Wow,' said Grace.

Quite.

A glass door led onto a sunny terracc straight out of *Homes and Gardens You'll Never in a Million Years Be Able to Afford*. Grace sat at the table under a classy cream parasol and tried desperately not to look too impressed, while Lou wandered round the garden, too jittery to sit still. It had been cleverly designed on a green and white theme. Elegant, Lou decided, but lacking in heart somehow. Personally she liked a bit more colour and chaos in a garden.

She was absently dead-heading some busy lizzies—white, of course—when Patrick and Tom eventually appeared, having clearly bonded without bothering with any introductions.

'I'm sorry about that.' At least Patrick had the grace to

sound a bit embarrassed at how long they had been. 'We got a bit carried away.'

Tom's face was glowing, not embarrassed at all. 'You should go and have a look, Mum,' he said eagerly. 'It's, like, a dream car! Patrick let me have a go with the gears. It's got *six*, and four-wheel drive, and guess what its top speed is?'

'Pretty fast, I should think.'

'A hundred and eight-nine miles per hour!'

'That's handy,' said Lou, wondering what was the point of a car that went at a hundred and eighty-nine miles an hour when the speed limit was seventy.

Grace was equally unimpressed, having heard her brother go on for hours about cars before. She let her elbow slip off the table and mimed falling asleep with boredom, but Tom wasn't to be deflated.

'It can go from nought to sixty-two miles an hour in four point two seconds,' he told his mother in a reverent tone, ignoring his sister. 'And when you're going really fast, these spoilers fold out and that gives you extra stability.'

'Spoilers? Really?' Lou didn't have a clue what her son was talking about, but she loved watching his face when he was lit up with enthusiasm like this. 'Jolly good.'

Patrick grinned at her expression. 'What's the betting your mother doesn't know what a spoiler is, Tom?'

'It's a kind of wing, Mum,' Tom explained kindly. 'It's sort of upside down. It folds out and keeps the car steady at speed. Patrick showed me. It's like the opposite of planes, isn't it, Patrick?' He was struggling a bit, obviously dying to show off his new knowledge but not that confident. 'You tell Mum,' he said to Patrick.

'Tom's right. Planes have wings designed to give them up force,' said Patrick obediently. 'On a high-performance car the wing is the other way, to keep them grounded. They generate so much force that you could drive a Formula One car upside down on a ceiling at two hundred miles an hour.'

Tom nodded eagerly. 'Can you imagine it?'

Frankly, Lou couldn't. Why would anyone want to drive upside down in the first place? Still, she appreciated that wasn't really the point.

'Wow,' she said dutifully, and then caught Patrick's eye. He was smiling, and looking so much more relaxed than she had ever seen him that she felt oddly hollow inside.

'I didn't realise that you were a petrol head too,' she said lightly to cover the sudden stumble of her heart.

'My mother always complained that cars were my only passion,' said Patrick cheerfully.

'I suppose they're less demanding than women,' said Lou in a dry voice, and he flashed a look at her.

'Exactly. I don't often meet anyone else who feels like I do about them, though. Tom knows a lot about cars,' he said, sounding genuinely impressed, and Lou felt herself flush with pleasure.

'He gets that from his father. Lawrie's mad about cars too.'

'Wait till I tell him I've been in a Porsche 911!' said Tom. 'He'll be really jealous.'

Much more jealous than he would be to hear that she was thinking of getting remarried, Lou couldn't help thinking.

'What about a drink?' said Patrick. 'Then we can have lunch. It's cold, so we just need to put it on the table.'

'Have you been slaving away in the kitchen all weekend?'

'My housekeeper has,' he admitted. 'She left it all for me yesterday.'

They ate in the kitchen, a bright, sunny room opening

out onto the terrace. Patrick said the dining room was too gloomy. 'I only use it for formal dinners.'

His housekeeper lived out, he told them, but had come in specially on Saturday to prepare the lunch, and she had done them proud, with a very simple but delicious spread.

'It must get a bit lonely rattling around in this great big house on your own, doesn't it?' said Lou, looking around her and calculating that they could probably fit their current flat into Patrick's kitchen alone.

'Only occasionally,' said Patrick. 'I'm out a lot.'

Ah, yes, with all those leggy blondes. Not a subject Lou wanted to raise in front of the children.

Fortunately Grace changed the conversation by asking Patrick if he had ever been skiing. 'I saw those photos of mountains in your loo,' she explained, and was soon telling him all about the trip she was so eager to go on, her sullen Goth pose quite forgotten.

'I wish I could go too,' said Tom enviously. 'Charlie's been snowboarding. He says it's really cool.'

'It sounds a great way to start,' Patrick said to Grace. 'When are you going?'

Grace's face closed as she remembered. 'I might not go at all,' she muttered. 'It's quite expensive. Mum's going to see what she can do, though.'

Patrick glanced across the table at Lou, who met his eyes for a moment before looking away. 'Could I have some more of that delicious salmon?' she said.

So that was why she had changed her mind, he thought, passing her the dish. Marrying him must have seemed the only way she could ever afford to send Grace on the trip she wanted so much.

It wasn't as if he hadn't known she would only consider marrying him for his money, Patrick reminded himself, puzzled by the slight pang he felt. Nobody could say she hadn't been honest with him. And that was what he wanted too. He didn't want a wife who would marry him because she loved him. That would just end in tears, the way all his other relationships did. He wanted it to be different with Lou.

There was something unfamiliar about her today. Patrick couldn't work out what it was until belatedly he realised that it was the first time he had seen her without one of her prim little suits she wore to work. Instead she had on cool linen trousers and a silky sleeveless top, with silver bangles on her wrist and silver drops hanging from her ears. She looked casual, but cool and elegant, and Patrick enjoyed the contrasting picture she made to her children, Grace with her outrageous outfit and wary charm, and Tom, hair standing up on end, still elated by encountering the car of his dreams.

The children lobbied for a swim after lunch. Lou's eyes followed Patrick as he led Grace and Tom off and showed them where they could change. It was very strange seeing the three of them together. Strange, too, to remember how nervous she had been about how they would get on. They all seemed fine, Lou thought. Bang went that excuse for not marrying him.

And now she had seen him with the children, she wasn't sure she wanted an excuse any more.

When Patrick came back, she was clearing away the lunch dishes.

'Leave all that,' he said. 'You go and sit in the garden. I'll bring you coffee.'

There was no doubt that it was nice to be looked after. Lou protested but Patrick was insistent, and in the end she wandered back out to the terrace as instructed. She paused for a moment to watch Tom and Grace splashing excitedly in the pool, then sat at the table with a little sigh. It was a perfect temperature under the parasol, with a soft breeze just ruffling the leaves, which fractured the sunlight. The whole garden seemed to sway with splashes of light and shade.

Lou watched a butterfly hovering by a white buddleia and breathed in the scent of the roses growing up the wall behind her. It was so quiet and peaceful here, the silence broken only by the shrieks from the pool. Incredible to think that they were right in the centre of London.

It would be easy to get used to this. Dangerously easy.

'What do you think of the garden?' Patrick asked, setting the coffee tray down on the table.

'It's lovely,' said Lou, looking around her.

A subtle change seemed to come over her when she was surrounded by plants, almost like a slackening of tension. Patrick had noticed it before, when he had come out of the bar and seen her sitting in the pub garden, her eyes closed and her face tipped back as she'd breathed in the scent of growing things, her mouth curved with pleasure.

He liked that about her, the way every now and then he got a glimpse of the secret, sensuous Lou who hid behind the practical façade and the prim suits and the cool, ironic gaze.

'I'm glad you said that,' he said, pouring out the coffee. 'I spent a fortune having it redesigned a couple of years ago.'

'It shows,' said Lou.

'Ouch,' said Patrick wryly. 'That wasn't the idea.'

'No, honestly, it's beautiful,' she said, trying to explain. 'It's just a bit too perfect for me, that's all.'

'Too perfect? That's a new one on me.'

'Well, you can tell that it's a garden that's been designed. It hasn't grown up gradually. It's not full of cuttings your neighbour has given you, or plants that have just put themselves in and are so determined to flower that you haven't got the heart to dig them up, even if they do clash with everything else.'

Lou gestured at the immaculate garden. 'There's no campanula running riot because you put it in without thinking a few years ago and it's now out of control.' A terrible thug in the garden, Fenny always said about campanula. 'I suppose it just doesn't seem like a garden that's loved,' she finished lamely.

Patrick looked at her curiously. She was always surprising him nowadays. 'I thought you would have liked everything neat and orderly, the way you keep things in the office.'

'No.' There was a pot of exquisite white lavender beside her, and Lou pulled a stem through her fingers. 'I like order in my life, but not in my gardens.' Lifting her hand to her nose, she sniffed the wonderful lavender fragrance. 'My perfect garden would be all jumbly and colourful, with plants tumbling everywhere, and thick with scent on a summer night…' She sighed wistfully, just thinking about it. One day…

'You're a romantic,' Patrick discovered, amused. 'I never had you down as one of those!'

Lou's face closed as she thought of Lawrie. 'I used to be. I'm not a romantic any more, though. You tend to lose your faith in romance when you've been through a divorce.'

'What happened?' asked Patrick, and then paused, wondering if he'd been tactless. 'Sorry, it's not my business.'

'No, it's OK.' He had told her why his marriage to Catriona had broken down, after all. 'If we're going to get married, it probably is your business anyway.'

Lou sipped her coffee, her eyes on the sunlight wavering

through the trees. 'It wasn't all a disaster. For a long time, we were really happy. I was happy, anyway.' She sighed a little. 'I was a real romantic then. I used to think that if you loved each other enough, nothing could go wrong, and I couldn't have loved Lawrie more. I loved him from the first moment I laid eyes on him.'

'Love at first sight?' Patrick looked sceptical. Lou wasn't surprised. Patrick was never going to be a love-at-first-sight kind of guy.

'I didn't believe in it either,' she said. 'Until it happened to me. One look, and I was lost. I'd never met anyone like Lawrie before. He was so good-looking and funny and he had charm oozing from every pore. I couldn't believe he'd look at a nice, sensible girl like me. He made me feel... wonderful...alive...*exciting*. He made me feel like I wasn't such a nice, sensible girl after all.'

Her eyes were alight with memories, her face soft and warm, and she smiled in spite of herself at the memory of those heady days.

Watching her, Patrick felt something stir inside him. Had he ever been able to make a woman glow like that, just thinking about him? It was a disquieting thought and he frowned down at his coffee.

'Of course, if I'd really been a sensible girl, I would never have married him,' Lou was saying. 'Being with Lawrie was like being on a roller coaster. One minute you were having the best fun you'd ever had, and the next you were in despair. He wouldn't call, he wouldn't turn up when he said he would, he'd be adoring you one minute and chatting up some other girl the next...'

She made a face remembering those bad times. 'Fenny said that I was mad to marry him, but I was besotted. It wasn't that I couldn't see Lawrie's faults, but none of them mattered against the fact that just being near him gave me the biggest thrill I'd ever known.'

'So what changed?' asked Patrick, vaguely disgruntled by all this. He was beginning to wish that he hadn't asked.

'I did.' A little of the warmth faded from Lou's face. 'It was great until Grace was born, but you have to think differently when you've got a baby to look after. You can't both be irresponsible and free spirits. Babies don't need excitement and romance, they need security and a routine, and Lawrie wasn't good at either of those. He didn't like feeling tied down by responsibility, and I didn't like not being able to count on him when it mattered.

'I could deal with it when it was just me,' she said. 'His unreliability was part of his charm, I suppose, but what made him fun and unpredictable as a lover was less endearing as a father. There were so many times when the children waited for him and he didn't turn up when he said he would, or looked forward to some treat he'd promised, which he changed his mind about at the last minute.'

'Disappointing for them,' said Patrick, thinking that Lawrie sounded a jerk. Why had Lou stuck with him for so long? She must have loved him a lot.

'Yes, nearly as disappointing as discovering that your husband has borrowed against the house to finance some wild scheme that's gone bust, so you've lost your home,' said Lou, her voice dusty dry. 'Or even being told that you're so boring and wrapped up in domesticity that he's decided to trade you in for a younger and more exciting model.'

'Why did you stay with him for so long?' demanded Patrick, angry for some reason.

'Because of the children. And because I loved him.'

'Are you still in love with him?'

Lou glanced at him, surprised at the harshness in his

voice. Patrick was surprised by it too. He hadn't meant to ask her that, but the question was out before he could stop it.

'I guess that isn't my business either,' he said.

Did she still love Lawrie? Lou twisted her coffee-cup in its saucer.

'I think part of me will always love him,' she said slowly. 'I can't imagine ever loving anyone else that deeply, and I don't want to. Lawrie hurt me so much in the end. I couldn't go through that again. I just couldn't,' she said. 'I'll never fall in love again. Not like that.'

She risked another glance at Patrick. He was looking a bit grim. Probably dreading an outburst of emotion.

'That's the only reason I could think about marrying you,' she told him. 'Knowing that you wouldn't expect me to love you, or even want me to.'

'No.' Patrick could hear the edge of doubt in his own voice, and he frowned. Where had that come from? 'No, I wouldn't,' he said more firmly. A bit too firmly, in fact. Almost as if he were protesting too much.

Fortunately Lou didn't seem to notice. 'And I wouldn't expect you to be faithful,' she said. 'I know you'd have other relationships, and I would accept that, of course.' She hesitated a little. 'The only thing is that I wouldn't want the children exposed to that fact. All I'd ask is that you were as discreet as you could be, and that you didn't bring any girlfriends back to the house if we were there.'

When she put it like that, the idea of carrying on a relationship when he was married to her sounded degrading somehow. Patrick shifted uncomfortably. Maybe it was a bit degrading. He hadn't really thought about how it would work in practice. He had just been determined to avoid emotional entanglements and keep all his options open. Wasn't that the whole point of marrying Lou?

But he certainly didn't want to hurt or humiliate her. How could she think that he would be that crass?

'I don't have a problem with that,' he said gruffly. 'I won't bring anyone back, I promise.'

'It looks like you might be able to have that fantasy of yours after all, then,' said Lou.

'Does this mean you're thinking about marrying me after all?'

She bit her lip. 'If you still want to.'

'Hey, you've just offered me my fantasy. How could I not want to?'

'Well, when you put it like that…' Lou tried to smile, but it didn't quite come off.

'The point is, do *you* want to?' said Patrick.

'I'm just worried about Grace and Tom. You were pretty clear that you weren't interested in being a stepfather, and I wouldn't be able to go through with it if I thought that you would resent them.'

'I wouldn't resent them,' said Patrick. 'I'd never thought about having kids around, that's all. But now that I've met them, I feel different. I didn't think I'd like them, to be honest, but I do.'

'You're not just saying that because Tom admired your car?'

He half smiled. 'No, it's not that.' He thought about it for a bit. 'I suppose they were just complications before, but now they're individuals. I can see now how important they are to you. I think I understand more why you'd be prepared to do this.'

They listened for a moment to the sound of Grace and Tom in the pool. There seemed to be a lot of shouting and splashing going on, thought Lou. They were obviously having a great time. When they had to entertain themselves and forgot to fight, the two of them got on very well.

'I don't suppose I would be a very touchy-feely stepfather,' Patrick said, 'but I would do my best. You want Grace to go skiing, don't you?'

'Yes,' said Lou in a low voice.

'She can go if you marry me. I can take Tom snowboarding if he wants to have a go at that. You can give them all the opportunities you want.' He paused. 'You could have your fantasy too, Lou. You wouldn't have to worry about things on your own any more. You'd have someone to talk to at the end of the day. You'd even have someone to hold you, if that was what you needed.'

Lou had been listening quietly, but her eyes jerked to his at that.

'As a friend,' Patrick clarified quickly. 'You've been frank about how you're not going to love me. Well, I won't love you either. We won't complicate things with sex.'

And it *would* be a complication, he thought. A quite unnecessary one too. Much better to put the whole idea out of his mind completely.

'We'd be partners,' he assured her. 'Friends rather than man and wife in the usual sense. We've got a chance here to make both our fantasies come true, Lou,' he said gently.

There was a pause. Lou watched a bee zooming over the thyme and thought about what Patrick had said. It all seemed to make such perfect sense when he talked like that. Why was she hesitating? Surely it couldn't be the way he had assured her that he wouldn't love her?

'Lou, I made a real mess of this before,' said Patrick after a while. 'Can I ask you again now?'

She nodded, her mind made up. 'Yes, ask me again.'

'Will you marry me, Lou?'

Lou took a breath and looked straight into his grey-green eyes. 'Yes,' she said. 'I will.'

CHAPTER SEVEN

THERE was an awkward pause as they looked at each other uncertainly. If they were a real couple, they would fall into each other's arms at this point, but clearly a passionate kiss wasn't appropriate in their case.

'We could shake hands on the deal,' Patrick suggested, making a joke of it. 'But it does seem a bit businesslike. I think we should kiss, don't you?'

Lou's heart did an alarming somersault at the very thought. 'Kiss?' she echoed, horrified at how squeaky her voice sounded.

'We may not be going to be lovers, but I hope we can be friends,' he said.

Right. A kiss between friends. That was all he meant.

Right. Calm down, Lou told her still-stuttering heart and firmly squashed a sneaky and quite irrational sense of disappointment. Friends, that was fine. She could do friends. She had been very clear that that was all she wanted, and she was glad that Patrick had got the message.

Very glad. Of course.

She cleared her throat to get rid of that ridiculous squeakiness. 'Sounds good to me,' she said, super casual.

'Good,' said Patrick, and leant across the table to kiss her on the cheek.

Lou had a dizzying sense of his nearness, and a sudden terrifying desire to turn her head and kiss him back, but it was over in a moment, and he was sitting back with a smile.

'Good,' he said again, looking across the table at Lou, and his smile widened. She looked somehow right, sitting there in his garden. He liked the idea that there would be other days when he would come home and find her here. The girls might come and go, but Lou would always be there. It was a good thought, and Patrick beamed with satisfaction. Everything was working out perfectly.

'Let's get married soon,' he said.

Lou swallowed nervously and decided to take the plunge. 'I want to talk to you both,' she said as she ladled baked beans onto toast. They had had such a good lunch that she thought she could get away with a Sunday-night snack.

'Baked beans? Great!' Tom sat up in his chair. 'My favourite,' he said excitedly, and Lou smiled in spite of her nerves. There had to be something to be said for a child whose tastes ranged from a car that even second-hand cost as much as a house to beans on toast.

'I hate beans,' said Grace, but she picked up her knife and fork anyway.

'There's something I want to say,' Lou began again as they started eating.

She couldn't face anything herself. She was too churned up at the decision she had made, and anxious about how the children would react.

Not to mention appalled at how shaky a mere kiss on the cheek had made her feel.

Patrick had suggested that they tell the children when they finally dragged them out of the pool, but Lou had wanted to do it on her own. So he had driven them home instead, putting the seal on Tom's day by letting him sit in the front passenger seat and play with all the buttons.

'Dad's got a sports car too,' he told Patrick. 'But it's not as good as this.'

The two of them talked cars while Lou and Grace were squeezed into the back seat. Sitting behind Tom, Lou found her eyes resting on Patrick's profile, on the strong neck and the line of his jaw and the sudden gleam of his smile that made her heart clench uncomfortably.

She had said that she would marry him.

She was going to *marry* him.

What had she let herself in for?

Panic, elation, terror and a weird kind of excitement churned around inside her at the thought, and she hardly noticed the drive across London until Patrick drew up outside the flat. Tom must have directed him.

It seemed unlikely that the neighbourhood had ever seen a car like this. 'I'd ask you up, but I don't think you should leave the car here,' Lou said nervously.

Patrick merely laughed. 'I'll see you tomorrow,' he said, and then he drove back to his fabulous house and his garden and his pool and Lou was left to make beans on toast.

'Earth to Planet Lou!' Grace waved a hand in front of her face. 'Wake up, Mum! You're weirding us out here.'

Weirding them out? Where did they get these expressions?

'Sorry.' Lou pulled herself together. 'Yes. So.' She cleared her throat. 'Um...did you enjoy today?'

'It was cool,' said Tom. 'I can't believe he's got a Porsche 911! I liked the pool too.'

'Yeah, the pool was great,' said Grace.

'And did you see that television?' Tom put in, and launched into a description of all its technical features before Lou cut him off.

'Forget about his things,' she said sharply. 'What about Patrick? Did you like him?'

Tom offered the ultimate accolade. 'He was really cool.'

Typically, Grace was less enthusiastic. 'He was OK,' she offered grudgingly. 'At least he didn't talk to us like we were children.'

Instead of the grown-ups they were at fourteen and eleven. Lucky Patrick had avoided that elementary error.

Still, he hadn't done badly to merit an OK. That was high praise from Grace.

'Well, I'm glad you liked him,' said Lou, squaring up to the challenge at last. 'That's what I want to talk to you about, actually. The thing is, Patrick and I are thinking of getting married.'

Lou often read about children wisely picking up on adult signals, but if she had hoped for a cosy admission from either of them that they had secretly suspected that Patrick was madly in love with her, she was due for a disappointment. Grace and Tom were dumbfounded.

They stared at her, their beans forgotten. 'You're kidding!'

'Er...no, I'm not, actually.'

'You mean *Patrick's* in love with *you*?' There was no mistaking the incredulity in Grace's voice. Lou couldn't blame her.

'No,' she said. She wanted to be honest with them. They deserved that at least. 'No, he isn't. And I'm not in love with him.'

At least she hoped she wasn't. She had certainly reacted very strangely to a little peck on the cheek. It might be a smidgeon of lust, perhaps, but love? No. She wasn't falling in love again. She had told Patrick that.

Lou paused, wondering how best to explain. 'Patrick and I aren't in love with each other, but we are friends, and we respect each other, and those things mean a good deal in a marriage. Ideally, we would love each other as well, but sometimes two out of three is good enough. I think we can have a strong, honest relationship.'

She was just confusing them, Lou could see. 'Look, if you don't like the idea, I won't marry him,' she tried to reassure them. 'Patrick knows that. The important thing is that the three of us are a family. We'd still be a family if I married Patrick, though. He'd just be there as well.'

'Would we still see Dad?' asked Tom anxiously.

'Of course you would. Patrick wouldn't try and be your father. He knows you've got your own dad. And it's not as if everything would change. You'd still go to the same school. We just wouldn't live here any more.'

'You mean we'd live in that house with a pool *all the time*?' Tom's eyes were huge.

'Well, yes, probably.'

Grace sat up straighter. 'Could I have my own room?'

'Yes, you could.'

'And go on that skiing trip?'

'Yes,' said Lou. 'You can go skiing.'

Grace looked at her mother for a long moment, and then she smiled. 'Thanks, Mum,' she said, and for some reason Lou felt tears prick her eyes.

'I know it will mean a big change for both of you,' she said, blinking them back fiercely. 'But nothing's going to change about *us*, I promise you. I know I've rather sprung this on you, and it may take you a bit of time to get used to the idea, but—'

'It's cool, Mum,' Tom interrupted her kindly. 'I don't want to be mean, but Patrick's house is a lot nicer than this. Living there will be better than living here, won't it?'

Lou looked around the poky kitchen, where the three of them were squeezed around the table. Upstairs, feet clomped across the ceiling, and the television blared from next door. Whenever she wondered if she'd made the right decision, she needed to remember this.

'Yes,' she said. 'It will.'

Lou stood on top of the hill and lifted her face to the wind. It was the end of July, mid-summer, but here high in the

Yorkshire Dales there was little sign of it. Grey clouds scudded across the sky, bringing the occasional splatter of rain, and the wind had a distinct chill to it.

Patrick poured coffee into the lid of a flask and handed it to her. Taking it, Lou sat next to him on a rocky outcrop and cradled the mug between her hands as she gazed down at the village below. She could see the river, the huddle of grey stone cottages around the sturdy church. Across the valley, half hidden in trees, was the hotel where they would be married the next day.

It had been a busy couple of months. Lou had thought it would be too difficult to carry on working for Patrick once they were married, so she had recruited a new PA for him and handed the office over in perfect order, not without a pang or two. She had plans to do a garden design course eventually, but it was sad leaving behind the people at Schola Systems who had been friends and colleagues for so long.

She had fewer regrets about leaving the flat. It was empty now, their things packed up and waiting for them in Chelsea. They were to move in with Patrick after the wedding, and life for all of them would change completely.

Patrick was obviously thinking about the future too. 'I can't believe we're actually going through with it,' he said, following her gaze to the hotel.

'It's not too late to change your mind,' she pointed out.

'What, and disappoint Fenny? I couldn't do it,' he said. 'She told me that she'd been hoping for years that you would find someone like me to marry!'

Lou had been relieved and more than a little surprised at her aunt's ready acceptance of Patrick. She wouldn't have thought that they would get on at all.

'I hope you appreciate what an honour that is,' she told

him, putting down her coffee to unwrap the packet of sandwiches Fenny had made for them that morning before ordering them out of the house. 'Fenny's like Grace. She doesn't give her approval easily.

'She never had any time for Lawrie,' Lou remembered, offering the sandwiches to Patrick. 'She told me that he had a weak chin and couldn't be trusted, and Lawrie thought that she was a rude and eccentric old woman. I used to have to come up to see her by myself. He flatly refused to come, and Fenny probably wouldn't have had him in the house anyway.'

Not wanting to have any secrets from her aunt, she had told Fenny the truth about her marriage to Patrick. She had expected her to be shocked and disapproving, but Fenny had merely listened carefully and nodded.

'Very sensible, dear,' was all she had said. 'You can get married from here as soon as the children break up for their summer holidays.'

Patrick brushed breadcrumbs from his trousers. 'Do *you* want to change your mind?' he asked carefully. 'I wouldn't blame you after being cornered by my mother last night.'

The two families had met for a pre-wedding party at the hotel, which had been virtually taken over by Patrick's sisters and their offspring. Grace and Tom had slotted effortlessly into the big group of nieces and nephews, one of whom had discovered the pool table. Lou had hardly seen them all evening.

She had liked Patrick's mother and sisters a lot. They were all down-to-earth and had teased Patrick mercilessly, unimpressed by his wealth.

'What on earth were the two of you talking about for so long?' he asked, taking another sandwich.

'You, of course,' said Lou. The wind was whipping her

dark hair around her face and she tried to hold it back with one hand while she ate her sandwich.

'I'd given up hope that Patrick would ever marry again,' Kate Farr told Lou when they found themselves on their own. 'The silly boy has been running around with quite unsuitable girls for far too long. I can't tell you how pleased I am that he's come to his senses at last and found himself a real woman!'

Lou couldn't help being amused at hearing Patrick roundly described by his mother as a 'silly boy', but she felt a little uncomfortable about the warm welcome she had received from his family. He obviously hadn't told his family the whole truth about their marriage.

'It's a shame that his father died when he did,' Kate was saying. 'Patrick was only fifteen, and I often think that he grew up too fast after that. And then there was Catriona. She was a nice enough girl,' she said fairly, 'but all wrong for Patrick. That marriage was never going to last. The divorce was supposedly amicable, but I know Patrick was much more hurt about it all than he wanted to admit.

'He threw himself into his work after that, and I think he made too much money too soon. That playboy lifestyle wasn't what he needed.' Kate shook her smartly coiffed grey head. 'He built up this image of Mr I-Don't-Care, but of course what he was afraid of was caring too much.'

'I know what that feels like,' Lou confessed and his mother studied her with eyes that were uncannily like her son's, and quite as shrewd.

'I thought you might,' she said. 'That's why you're right for him. I just hope that you know that much of what Patrick shows the world is just a façade. Underneath he's generous and dependable, and he's got a kind heart. Nothing's too much trouble for the few people he really cares about. You know that, don't you?'

Lou looked across at Patrick, and felt something shift inside her. He was surrounded by his sisters, laughing and throwing up his hands in defeat as if resigned to being the butt of their jokes. It was hard to recognise the cold, hard man she hadn't wanted to have dinner with in Newcastle.

'Yes,' she said to his mother, 'I know.'

She was pretty sure that if she asked him, he would do anything for her or the children, just as Kate said. But he would do it because they had signed a pre-nuptial contract to say that he would.

Lou wanted him to do it because he cared for them too.

And that wasn't in the contract.

The grey clouds cleared miraculously for Lou's wedding day. She woke to sunshine pouring through the bedroom window and a knot of nerves in her stomach. A perfect summer day. A perfect day to get married.

If only you were marrying a man who loved you.

Lou's fingers shook as she laid out her outfit. There had been no question of a white dress—the wedding was going to be enough of a fraud as it was—and she had chosen a pale pink suit to wear with the string of pearls Fenny had given her.

'I'd like you to wear these at your wedding,' she had said, unwrapping the velvet cloth in which the pearls had lain unworn for years.

'Oh, Fenny, they're beautiful!' Lou held them against her skin, admiring their warm lustre.

'My neck's too scraggy to wear them now,' said Fenny. 'And they're not really suitable for gardening, which is all I do nowadays.' She put her head on one side to study Lou who was fastening the pearls around her neck. 'Donald gave them to me when we were married, so goodness knows how long ago that is now... It certainly makes them something old for you to wear with your wedding outfit, anyway! I'd like you to have them.'

Marisa had approved. 'I've brought some pearl earrings to lend you that'll go perfectly with Fenny's necklace,' she announced, breezing into the room as Lou was getting changed. She had insisted on coming to help Lou dress, in spite of everything Lou had to say about it not being a proper wedding.

'So now you've got something old and something borrowed,' she said, picking up a lipstick from the dressing table. 'I trust you've bought yourself some new underwear at least for today, so all you need is something blue.' She pulled the top off the lipstick and frowned. 'I hope you're not planning to wear this with that suit, are you?'

'I bought it specially,' Lou protested.

Marisa was shocked. 'It's far too pale! You need something much brighter than that. I'll see what I can find.' She dug in her bag for the vast cosmetic case she never travelled without. 'Are you OK, Lou? It's not like you to make a mistake when it comes to style!'

'I'm nervous.' Lou fiddled edgily with the pearls. 'What if I'm doing the wrong thing?'

Marisa put the cosmetic case on one side and concentrated on Lou. 'OK, what could go wrong?' she asked patiently.

'Everything! The children might not get on with Patrick; he might not get on with them.'

'They seem to get on fine at the moment.'

'They do now, but what if Patrick gets bored with us? He might meet some...some *supermodel* with no bottom and legs up to her armpits and decide he wants to have babies with her!' said Lou wildly.

'I agree Patrick's more likely to meet a supermodel than most men,' Marisa conceded, 'but if he'd wanted to marry someone like that, he could have done. It's you he's marrying.'

'Yes, but not for the right reasons,' said Lou wretchedly. 'If it all goes wrong, I'll have given my children an absolutely terrible example of how to form adult relationships, won't I?'

Marisa sighed. 'I hate to be tactless, but that low life Lawrie isn't exactly a shining role model when it comes to relationships, and you married *him*.'

'All the more reason not to make the same mistake again. Shouldn't I be teaching the children about adults loving each other, not making deals?'

'It's always a deal, Lou,' said Marisa stringently. 'Yes, you've made a deal, but it's an open and honest one. It's a good start—and who's to say that you and Patrick won't come to love each other?'

Lou shook her head. 'No, we're not going to do that,' she said. 'I told you, we've agreed that's not what either of us want.'

'Well, it seems a sinful waste to me.' Her friend sighed. 'I can't believe you haven't noticed how attractive he is. I wouldn't be letting any ditzy blondes get their paws on him if he was mine!'

Lou turned away to pick up the pearls. 'I don't want to get hurt again,' she said. 'I'd rather he hurt the blondes.'

'If I were you, I'd just relax and see what happens,' Marisa advised. 'I don't think Patrick would hurt you, anyway.'

'You can't know that.'

'Well, I told him that if he *did* hurt you, I would personally come after him with a pair of shears—and it wouldn't just be the sleeves of his suits I'd be chopping off!'

Lou couldn't help laughing and immediately felt better. 'Poor Patrick! What did he say?'

'Very sensibly, he said that he wouldn't.' Marisa grinned and made a scissoring gesture with her fingers. 'But he has been warned!'

Once the knotty question of the lipstick had been sorted out, Marisa insisted on bringing Lou a glass of champagne. Lou was doubtful at first.

'It was champagne that got me into this mess in the first place!'

'Hey, you're marrying a millionaire,' said Marisa. 'You're also getting married for the second time, when some of us are still looking for a guy to waltz us up the aisle once, let alone twice. Don't knock it!'

Grace sidled into the room when she was gone in search of a bottle. Lou swung round on the dressing-table stool, her heart squeezing at the sight of her daughter who had eschewed her normally gloomy wardrobe for a pretty mint-green dress covered in pink dots. On her feet she wore pink ballerina shoes in place of her usual clumpety black boots.

Lou had told her that she could wear whatever she wanted, and she had been very touched when Grace had opted for a dress that she had known would please her mother. She had even brushed her hair.

'You look lovely,' said Lou sincerely.

'Thanks. You look nice too, Mum,' Grace muttered. She brought a hand out from behind her back. 'Marisa says you need something blue.'

It was a perfectly hideous bracelet, made up of blue plastic cubes on an elasticated band, but Lou knew how treasured it was. A boy at school, about whom Grace was unusually coy, had given it to her the previous Christmas.

'You can wear this if you want.'

It was a real sacrifice, Lou knew, and her throat was tight

as she got up and hugged her daughter. 'Thank you, Grace. I'd love to wear it.'

Grace was not normally a tactile child, but she clung to her mother for a moment. 'I just wanted to say thank you,' she said in a rush. 'I know you're doing this for me, and for Tom.'

Lou held her close, her heart full. 'I'm doing it for all of us, Grace,' she told her quietly. 'Everything's going to be fine.'

Stepping back with a smile, she slipped the bracelet onto her wrist. It threw out all Marisa's style rules, and her friend would have a fit when she saw it, but it meant more to Lou than anything else that day.

'I'll take great care of it,' she promised Grace.

Afterwards, Lou remembered little of the wedding itself. The simple ceremony was held in the garden of the hotel, and, although they had decided just to invite family..and Marisa, who was an honorary member of the family, as Fenny pointed out...there seemed to be a lot of people grouped around them and smiling.

As they waited for the celebrant to gather her thoughts together and begin, Lou saw Patrick's mother, who had pulled out all the stops with an imposing hat, before her eyes skipped on to Fenny, eccentrically dressed in a striped dress that had to be at least thirty years old. Then there was Grace, and Tom, his shirt tail already hanging loose, and Marisa, who gave her a discreet thumbs-up sign.

Lou managed a smile for them all, and then she turned to Patrick and everything else faded into a vague background. It was as if the rest of the party were no more than a blur of faces and figures, cut off from the two of them by an invisible barrier.

Only Patrick was real and solid. He looked very smart in a grey suit, an immaculate white shirt, and a pale grey tie. Lou found herself staring at his face as if she had never seen him properly before. That jaw, that cool, firm mouth, the hard line of his cheek…had he always looked like that?

Her gaze travelled over him as if fascinated until her eyes reached his. Light, more green than grey today, and somehow disturbing, they held a quizzical smile at her scrutiny, and Lou blushed as she looked quickly away.

The celebrant cleared her throat. 'Shall we start?' she asked in an undertone, and Patrick turned to face her. After a moment's hesitation, Lou did the same.

Getting married was a strange experience this time. She heard the words, and made the right responses, marvelling at the steadiness of her own voice, but part of her didn't seem to be there at all. It was like watching herself in a film.

Then Patrick was taking her hand, sliding the ring onto her finger and suddenly it all felt horribly real. His fingers were warm and sure, and Lou felt herself go hollow inside at his touch. Her own hands shook slightly as she picked up the ring to push it onto Patrick's finger, but at last it was done.

They were married.

Patrick smiled and turned to Lou quite naturally, putting his hand under her chin and lifting her face so that he could kiss her. At the touch of his mouth the ground seemed to drop away beneath Lou's feet. His lips weren't cool, the way she had imagined them to be. They were warm and firm and dangerously exciting, and her heart jolted in response. Unable to resist it, Lou leant slightly into him, and Patrick's mouth lingered on hers for a moment longer than necessary before he forced himself to lift his head.

She looked almost as startled as he felt. Patrick felt ridiculously shaken by the unexpected sweetness of that one kiss. He couldn't believe such a brief gesture could have thrown him so off balance, or what an effort it was to muster a flippant smile.

'Well, we did it,' he said.

'Yes,' said Lou, and smiled a little uncertainly back at him.

Patrick was conscious of a sudden urge to pull her back into his arms, but she was already turning, her smile widening as Grace and Tom reached her. He watched as she hugged them both to her, aware of a feeling that it took him a little while to identify as jealousy. Just because Lou loved her children and they loved her and got to be gathered close into her softness and her warmth whenever they wanted her or needed her.

How pathetic was it to feel jealous about *that*?

Patrick suddenly realised that Grace was smiling tentatively at him, and he pulled himself together. He opened his arms, and to his surprise she stepped into them for a quick, hard hug. 'Thank you, Grace,' he said, meaning it. He had known her long enough to know that Grace only hugged the people who meant most to her, and he felt a sudden rush of pride and pleasure to be included.

Ruffling Tom's hair, he glanced over at Lou and found her watching him with her children. The expression in her dark eyes was impossible to read, but she smiled at him, and Patrick felt something unlock inside him. He longed suddenly to be alone with her, the way they had been on top of that hill yesterday, but there was no chance of that with all these people here, all wanting to congratulate him and kiss Lou.

And things didn't get any better. At one point in the afternoon, it seemed to Patrick that he was the only one not getting to kiss the bride. It was hard to get near her. He kept getting glimpses of her dark head and her warm smile and then somebody else would come up and want him to be pleasant to them.

Patrick grew more and more frustrated. 'Don't worry, you'll get her to yourself soon enough,' his elder sister said, coming up behind him. She laughed at his disconcerted expression. 'We're all enjoying the sight of you besotted at last. You haven't been able to take your eyes off Lou all day.'

Besotted? He wasn't besotted, Patrick thought crossly. What a ridiculous idea. He had never been besotted with anyone in his life. Everyone knew that he was the one who ran a mile at the faintest hint of emotion. It was just a groom's job to keep an eye on his bride, that was all.

Unthinkingly, he sought Lou in the crowd. She was standing with his mother and Fenny, and they were all laughing. Lou's face was alive, her dark eyes sparkling, and his chest felt suddenly tight.

She looked wonderful in that suit, so different from the demure grey ones she wore to the office. The soft pink colour made her skin glow, and the silk jacket was fastened low to offer a glimpse of something that looked as if it were made of satin and lace beneath. The mere thought of it was enough to make Patrick catch his breath.

With those high-heeled shoes, she looked incredibly sexy, yet elegant at the same time. Patrick wasn't sure where the blue plastic bracelet fitted into the colour scheme, but it looked OK to him. Today Lou could carry off anything.

He *wasn't* besotted. He just wished that he were with her. Just wished that they were alone and that he were the one making her laugh. Wished that he could undo that jacket and find out just what she was wearing underneath…

Patrick swallowed.

'Besotted,' his sister confirmed with satisfaction. 'It was

about time you fell in love with a real woman, instead of all those bimbos you've been running around with for all this time, trying to prove that you weren't going to be middle-aged like the rest of us. Talk about an extended mid-life crisis. Oh, there's Michael!' She waved at a man through the crowd. 'I must go and have a word.'

Patrick was left outraged by his sister's candid remarks. He had not been trying to prove anything, he had never had any suggestion of a mid-life crisis and he most certainly wasn't in love with Lou.

In spite of himself, he glanced her way again. She was bending down to talk to one of his small nieces. He could see the way her breasts moved beneath that jacket, the way the silky dark hair swung against her cheek, the way she smiled with those lips that had tasted so piercingly, unexpectedly sweet. Patrick's head reeled and he closed his eyes briefly.

He was *not* in love with his wife.

A bit in lust, maybe, but that was all it was.

He was just frustrated. He hadn't had so much as a date since he and Lou had agreed to marry. Lou had made it clear that she would have no objections, but somehow Patrick hadn't felt like going out.

That would have to change. Lou had been definite that a physical relationship was out, and in any case Patrick had no intention of closing off his options with other women. That was the whole reason he had married her in the first place!

No, forget Lou's camisole, he told himself sternly. Stick with friendship, just as they had agreed before she'd started putting on pink suits and kissing him.

Patrick was glad now that he had got his new PA to arrange suites at all the hotels they were going to stay at on their way back to London. It hadn't seemed appropriate to book a honeymoon, but he had suggested that they make their way home slowly, visiting some gardens on the way if that appealed to Lou.

'But you're not interested in gardens,' she had protested.

'No, but I am interested in my car. I'll be happy to drive all the way.'

Lou laughed. 'Ah, now I understand!'

'All the hotels have got suites,' he added casually, 'so you should be quite comfortable. You'll be able to have a room of your own every night.'

She didn't even hesitate. 'Great,' she said. 'Thanks for organising that.'

So that was fine. Separate beds all the way. Patrick sneaked another glance at Lou.

It was fine by him too. Absolutely fine.

CHAPTER EIGHT

IT WAS nearly seven before Patrick and Lou managed to say all their goodbyes. The roof was down as they drove off into a golden summer evening, and the car seemed to float along the winding dales roads. It should have been an idyllic start to a honeymoon, thought Lou, leaning her head back against the plush leather seat.

Only it wasn't a proper honeymoon, of course. They were just going to stay the night at a couple of hotels on their way back to London. There would be no intimate celebrations, no elation, no laughter, no kisses.

No making love.

Patrick had made it very clear that they wouldn't be sharing a room, let alone a bed. That was fine by her, Lou reminded herself firmly, but it did make the whole notion of a honeymoon a bit of a mockery. They might just as well have driven back with Grace and Tom, but Lawrie had, for once, turned up as arranged to collect them from the reception. The children were going to spend a week with him. It was good for them to see their father, Lou thought, but it did mean that she was now going to have to spend a week alone with Patrick.

Of course, they had spent plenty of time alone in the office, but it was different now. Lou stole a sideways glance at Patrick. Her *husband*. She still couldn't quite comprehend it.

His expression was preoccupied, but his hands were very sure on the steering-wheel. As she watched he shifted gear to round a tight bend, completely in control of the powerful car, and something tightened and twisted inside Lou. Something deep and disturbing. Something that brought back the memory of the kiss they had shared after the ceremony in a vivid whoosh, so that she could feel again the warmth of his lips, the touch of his hand against her face.

Awareness of him shivered through her, vibrating out to her fingertips and toes, and Lou had to force herself to look away. Feeling like this whenever you looked at your husband was fine, but not when you and your husband had agreed very clearly that there was no question of a physical relationship. It was just as well that Patrick had arranged separate rooms while they were away.

It took them less than an hour to reach the hotel he had booked for that night, and the manageress came out to give them her personal attention. 'You must allow me to congratulate you both, Mr and Mrs Farr,' she said unctuously as they checked in. 'I understand you were just married today.'

Patrick looked up sharply from signing the form. 'How do you know that?'

She checked her notes. 'A...let me see, yes...Marisa Brandon...rang up earlier. She wanted to arrange for us to put a bottle of champagne in the suite for you to enjoy when you got here, and she mentioned that you would be coming straight from your wedding, so of course we're absolutely delighted to move you to our special honeymoon suite. It's just been renovated and completely refurbished to create a really special intimate and romantic atmosphere.'

Patrick glanced at Lou, but she shook her head very slightly to indicate that he shouldn't insist on the original arrangement. She certainly didn't want to stand there while he explained that actually they would rather have separate rooms. Some honeymoon they would seem to be on then!

The manageress insisted on escorting them up to the honeymoon suite, talking proudly about it all the way.

'I do hope you'll like it,' she said, opening the door for them. 'It's the perfect place for a honeymoon, I think.'

'It's lovely,' said Lou dutifully, and tried not to look at the bed. There was just the one, naturally. How many honeymoon suites catered for couples who didn't want to sleep together on their wedding night?

She would kill Marisa when she saw her.

'Well,' she said when the manageress had finished her tour of the suite, evidently designed to ensure that they appreciated every last intimate and romantic detail, and had at last left them alone.

'I'm sorry about this,' said Patrick. 'This isn't quite what I planned.'

'It doesn't matter,' said Lou, who had been thinking about the situation while listening to the manageress with half an ear. 'It won't kill us to share a bed for one night,' she went on briskly. 'There's no need to be silly about it. Look, it's huge,' she said, pointing at the bed.

Yes, and what a great bed it would be to make love in, thought Patrick, and was immediately cross with himself for being able to imagine doing just that.

'There's plenty of room for both of us,' Lou was saying, determined to show that the situation didn't bother her in the slightest. 'I don't see why it should be uncomfortable. We've both agreed that our relationship is going to be about friendship and nothing else, and if we *are* going to be friends, we should be able to share a bed without making a fuss.'

Her matter-of-fact attitude was beginning to annoy Patrick. So she wasn't bothered by the idea of sharing a bed with him. That didn't help *him*, did it? Lou obviously hadn't spent most of the day speculating about what he was wearing underneath *his* jacket. If she had, she might find the prospect of climbing into bed with him a lot more problematic.

Well, he would just have to show that he could be equally cool.

'Right, well, if you're happy with that, it's fine by me,' he said, a little too heartily. 'But I'm quite happy to go and have a quiet word down at Reception to see if they can give us back the original suite.'

'There's no need for that.' Lou sat down on the edge of the bed and eased off her shoes, just to prove how totally and utterly relaxed she was about the whole idea of sleeping with Patrick. 'Now that we're married, we're likely to find ourselves in this situation again, so we'd better get used to it.'

Patrick opened the fridge bar. 'In that case, we might as well have some of this champagne Marisa has provided for us.' He could certainly do with a drink.

Massaging her sore feet, Lou watched him surreptitiously as he deftly opened the bottle. Patrick seemed convinced by her show of unconcern, even if her insides weren't. Her entrails were clearly still very dubious about the whole business, and were churning and fluttering frantically at the mere prospect of climbing calmly into bed with him.

Patrick poured out the champagne and put the two glasses down by the bed while he pulled off his tie. Loosening his shirt at the neck, he rolled up his sleeves, took off his shoes and swung his legs up onto the bed so that he could make himself comfortable against the pillows.

'That's better,' he said, adjusting a pillow behind him. 'At least we can relax now.'

Well, *he* might be able to relax, thought Lou, still perched prissily on the edge of the bed. He was used to sharing beds with the likes of Ariel Harper.

And that meant that he was hardly likely to be overcome by lust at the idea of *her* on the other side of the bed, was he? Lou reminded herself, and her churning entrails quietened a little. Really, she was just being silly. She was forty-five, for heaven's sake. Far too old to be getting in a state about something so ridiculous.

So when Patrick patted the other side of the bed and urged her to put her feet up, Lou calmly scooted up onto the pillows beside him. He gave her a glass of champagne before picking up his own.

'Here's to us,' he said, toasting her.

'To us and our deal,' she agreed as they chinked glasses.

Not that the deal was going to be much comfort to him that night, Patrick reflected grimly. It looked like being a very long night.

And it *was* a long night. It was all very well reminding yourself that you were grown up, and far too old to be embarrassed about something so silly, but somehow that didn't help very much when you had to contemplate taking your clothes off and climbing into bed together.

Feeling about sixteen, Lou shut herself in the bathroom to change into the silk nightdress Marisa had given her as a mock wedding present. 'You might as well look good on your honeymoon, even if you are just going to sleep,' she had said.

If only it weren't quite so obviously made for seduction. Lou regarded herself in the bathroom mirror in dismay. The creamy oyster silk was a cool ripple against her skin, with a plunging back held up by whisper-light straps that were just begging for the brush of a man's hand to send them slithering off her shoulders. It felt lovely, it looked lovely, it was perfect for a sophisticated honeymoon. She just wished that it were a high-necked flannelette nightgown like the ones Fenny sometimes wore in winter.

Holding her clothes in front of her to hide as much of it as possible, Lou took a deep breath before walking out of the bathroom with assumed nonchalance. 'The bathroom's all yours,' she said casually over her shoulder, managing not to look at him at all as she put her clothes away.

'Thanks.'

By the time Patrick came out, she was lying on her side in the bed, the duvet pulled primly up under her chin. She had left a lamp burning on his side, but otherwise the room was in darkness, much to Patrick's relief. He always slept naked, so it had never occurred to him to buy pyjamas, but he had done his best to preserve the decencies by keeping his shorts on. Still, he was very glad Lou's eyes weren't on him as he crossed over to the bed. That glimpse of her bare back emerging from oyster silk had done alarming things to his blood pressure.

The mattress shifted as he got into bed and switched off the light. 'Goodnight,' he said gruffly.

'Goodnight.'

Oh, yes, it was all very polite. They were adults. They could deal with this. But it didn't stop Patrick being burningly aware of her, while, a few inches away, Lou could hear him breathing. It was so long since she had shared a bed that she was aware of every move he made as he stretched and settled in a studiedly relaxed way.

Long minutes ticked past. They weren't touching at all, but it was stifling under the duvet. Lou eased it off, kicking her legs free as quietly as she could, and cursing the long silk that kept tangling round her. She was longing to turn over, but she was terrified of brushing against Patrick—not that he would probably notice now. She could tell from the change in his breathing that he had fallen asleep. It was all right for some, she thought sourly.

She was exhausted, but too tense to sleep, and it felt as

if she lay there for hours, willing herself to relax. Then, just as she drifted off, she would jerk awake as Patrick sighed or stirred.

She was cold, too, now, but somehow the duvet had ended up all on Patrick's side. Lou tugged at it as discreetly as she could, and finally managed to get enough to cover herself once more, only to find to her horror that she had roused Patrick from the depths of his slumber. Rolling over, he flung a heavy arm over her and pulled her back into the warmth of his body so that he could nuzzle her neck, and Lou's attempts to wriggle free only made him tighten his grip in instinctive response.

'Patrick!' she said at last, and jabbed him with her elbow.

Waking with a start, Patrick took a moment or two to remember where he was and what he was doing. When he did, he recoiled as if he had found himself cuddling a black mamba. 'Sorry,' he muttered as he rolled hastily back to the other side of bed. 'I must have thought...'

'It's OK,' said Lou, not wanting to know who he had thought that she was. 'Go back to sleep.'

Fat chance of that when he had been pressed against her softness and his face had been buried in her hair and he had breathed in the warm fragrance of her skin! Patrick spent the rest of the night lying grim and rigid on the edge of the mattress, and trying not to remember how it had felt to wake holding her.

They didn't have to share a room again, and that made things much easier. No more lying stiffly on one side of the bed in case he rolled against her inadvertently. No more thinking about how close she was, or how easy it would be to reach out for her, to snuggle up like spoons the way he had before.

And what a mistake *that* would have been, Patrick told himself constantly. That would have been the end of his free and easy lifestyle, the end of beautiful girls, the end of freedom.

So he couldn't get Lou's warm body out of his mind? So he kept thinking about how luminous her skin had seemed in the dim light, and the curve of her shoulder in the darkness? He would get over it as soon as they got home and things went back to normal.

In meantime, they were friends, and that was fine.

Both were heartily glad when their supposed honeymoon was over and they could try and establish a new routine in London. Patrick went back to work with his new PA, and Lou stayed in the big, empty house and tried not to miss him. Things were better when the kids came back from Lawrie's. They loved living with Patrick, and the pool was a huge draw, especially while the summer holidays lasted and the house was always full of their friends, who spent the whole day splashing around and shouting.

There wasn't much for Lou to do, though. 'How are things in the office?' she asked almost wistfully when Patrick came home.

'OK,' he said, but without much enthusiasm. 'Jo's very efficient, but she's not like you.' He looked at Lou, who was cutting back the wisteria that was running rampant over the back of the house. 'It's funny without you there,' he said slowly. 'I miss you.'

Lou kept snipping at the top of her ladder. There was no need to start glowing just because he had said he missed her.

'I miss working with you more than I expected to,' she confessed. 'All those years commuting and longing not to have to work any more, and, now that I don't, I feel at a bit of a loose end. I'm quite glad Theresa's left now. At least I can keep house now. When she was here, I always felt awkward about going into the kitchen.'

Patrick sat down at the table and stretched his long legs out in front of him as he watched Lou cutting back the tendrils that were rioting away from the wires designed to keep the plant flat against the brick wall.

'It's all very quiet,' he said, suddenly realising that the pool lay silent and gleaming in the evening light. 'Where are the kids?'

'They're both on sleepovers with friends,' said Lou as she climbed cautiously down the ladder.

'Odd how empty the house feels without them,' said Patrick.

It was extraordinary, he thought, how quickly he had got used to coming home to noise and what seemed like perpetual motion. There always seemed to be a pack of kids running around, or splashing and shouting in the pool. The television would be going in one room, a CD of strange music Patrick had never heard before blasting from another. It had used to be such a quiet house too, he remembered. Quiet and very dull, now that he came to think about it. No wonder he had spent most evenings out.

Nowadays he found himself coming home earlier and earlier. He could bank on finding Lou in the garden, usually on her knees as she weeded and pruned and watered. Patrick had grown to like the way she looked up at him and smiled a welcome. She would sit back on her heels and brush the hair from her face, leaving a smudge on her forehead.

Most evenings they would sit together on the terrace and talk over a glass of wine. It felt very comfortable being with Lou, Patrick thought, and was glad that they had opted just to be friends. Later they would have supper in the kitchen with Grace and Tom, often with an assortment of other children whose names Patrick never established. The summer holidays were particularly chaotic, but Lou was always serene in the heart of it all. She seemed to know what was going on and who was going where, and after a while Patrick relaxed and left it all to her.

It had all worked out better than he had imagined, he congratulated himself. Now and then he would remember the other life that he had planned for himself, but it was puzzling now to know how that would have worked. He had been going to have a completely detached existence, hadn't he? The idea was to go out with other women with a guilt-free conscience, and to have nothing much to do with Lou and certainly not with her children. Patrick had been so sure then that was what he wanted.

Now…now it was different somehow.

He looked at Lou as she pulled off her gardening gloves and brushed wisteria leaves from her hair. She was wearing a faded shirt and the loose trousers she kept for gardening, and her hands were grubby. For an incongruous moment he remembered his cool, immaculate PA in her neat suits, but it was hard to reconcile her with the warm, slightly dishevelled woman who stood in front of him now.

'It's just us tonight, then?' he said.

'I'm afraid so.' Lou reached for a brush and began to sweep up the wisteria trimmings.

'Why don't we go out to dinner?' Patrick asked her on the spur of the moment, and she sent him a quick glance before bending back to her sweeping.

'You don't need to entertain me,' she said carefully. 'I'm fine on my own. Why don't you take Ariel out instead?'

Ariel? It took Patrick a moment to remember who she was talking about. 'Didn't I tell you? Ariel's gone back to the Maldives.'

Lou looked up from her broom. 'Really?'

'Apparently she met some diving instructor or something while we were there, and now she's decided that she wants to marry him and have babies. Whether he'll be able to keep her in the manner to which she is undoubtedly accustomed is another matter,' said Patrick in a dry voice.

'Are you OK with that?' asked Lou cautiously. He certainly sounded OK, but with Patrick you could never tell.

'Of course,' he said, surprised. 'I was just glad to be spared a horrible emotional scene when we came back. She'd made up her mind even then. To be honest, I'd forgotten all about her until you mentioned her.'

Lou bent to brush the leaves into a dustpan and dumped them in a wheelbarrow. 'Haven't you found anyone else to catch your fancy?' she said, determinedly casual and friendly. It was the kind of thing she would ask Marisa, after all. She and Patrick were friends, and asking how the other's love life was going was part of what friends did.

'No,' said Patrick slowly, realising that it was true. 'No, not yet.'

'Well, I don't mind being taken out until you find a new date,' said Lou, determinedly cheerful. 'I'll need to shower, though.'

'There's no hurry.'

Patrick had to force himself not to imagine Lou in the shower as he flicked through his organiser for the number of a restaurant. There were any number of trendy restaurants where he was pretty sure of getting a table, but it was hard to picture Lou in them. They were the kind of places you took glamorous girls like Ariel who cared about seeing and being seen. Lou wouldn't be bothered with any of that, he just knew.

'We're not going anywhere too smart, are we?' Lou called down the stairs, as if reading his mind.

Patrick went out into the hall and craned his neck to see her hanging over the banister from the landing. Her hair was wet, her shoulders bare above the cream towel she had wrapped around her, and she looked pink and glowing.

And alarmingly desirable. Patrick wondered what it would be like to be able to climb the stairs towards her and tell her how she looked. What would it be like if she smiled at the expression in his eyes and reminded him that they had the house to themselves for once? Would she laugh as he pulled her into the bedroom? Would she fall with him onto the bed? Would she let him unwrap her, unlock her, let his hands drift over her curves as he savoured the texture of her skin, the taste of her, the touch of her?

No, she wouldn't. Patrick reeled his wayward thoughts abruptly back. Of course she wouldn't. That wasn't the kind of thing you did when you were just friends, was it?

'Where would you like to go?' he asked, aware that his voice was hoarser than usual.

'Let's just go to that little Italian round the corner,' said Lou. 'It's always good there and we won't need to book. I'll be down in just a minute,' she assured him, disappearing from view.

Patrick went into the sitting room and sat on one of the sofas, dropping his head into his hands. He had to stop thinking about Lou like that, or one of these days he would forget himself, and that would spoil everything. It was only now that he was realising how important she was to him, and he didn't want to lose her as a friend. He was happy with how things were, and Lou seemed happy too, but that would only last if he stuck to the deal they had agreed.

So stick with it he would. And he would find a new girlfriend, the sooner the better.

'Are you OK, Patrick?'

Patrick jerked his head up to see Lou looking at him in concern from the doorway. She was wearing a pale blue silky skirt and a white top, with a soft little cardigan, and she looked cool and fresh and comfortable.

And just as desirable as she had looked wrapped in that towel.

Patrick swallowed hard and got to his feet. 'I'm fine,' he said brusquely. 'Let's go.'

'Brewer's First are having a big bash to mark their fiftieth anniversary at the end of September,' he told Lou over a bowl of pasta. 'We're both invited.'

'Do you want me to come and do my corporate-wife act?' asked Lou.

'Would you mind?'

'Of course not. I haven't done anything to keep my side of the bargain yet.' She smiled at him. 'I haven't forgotten our deal.'

'Good.' Patrick looked away, but her smile still shimmered behind his eyelids. He cleared his throat. 'Good.'

'Will it be a very posh affair?' Lou asked after a moment, a little puzzled by his silence. 'Should I dress up?'

'It's black tie, so you'll need evening dress, yes. Why don't you buy yourself something new?'

Lou ran a mental eye over her wardrobe. She didn't have anything very exciting, but there were a few basics she could easily glam up. 'I'm sure I can find something suitable at home,' she told him.

'You never buy yourself anything new,' said Patrick abruptly. 'I've noticed. You're still wearing the same clothes you had before we were married.'

'There's nothing wrong with them, is there?'

'It's not that.' He hunched a shoulder, obscurely hurt but not wanting to admit it. 'It's like you don't want to spend any of my money,' he explained as best he could. 'You hardly touch the money I put in your account.'

'I use it for food,' she protested.

'It's your money,' he said irritably. 'You don't need to account to me for what you do with it. Buy whatever you want.'

Lou set her jaw stubbornly. 'I don't feel comfortable about doing that,' she said and Patrick rolled his eyes.

'I thought you married me for my money!'

'I married you for security,' she said evenly. 'For a better life for me and the kids, and you've given us that. You have no idea what it's like living in that beautiful big house after that flat we were in. We don't need your money as well.'

'Try and spend some of it anyway,' said Patrick with an exasperated sigh. 'Buy yourself a new dress for that reception—and don't you dare buy anything cheap because you think it's not your money!' he added with a stern look. 'You'll be there as my wife, and I don't want you to give the impression that I'm tight-fisted!'

Lou rang Marisa the next morning. 'Patrick's practically ordered me to go and squander a fortune on a dress,' she said. 'You'd better come and help me choose.'

'Ooh, he didn't wake you up by waving a credit card in front of your face and telling you that you had shopping to do, did he?' said Marisa enviously. 'That's been my fantasy ever since I saw *Pretty Woman*!'

'No, but it feels a bit as if I'm being bought,' Lou confessed. 'I don't like it.'

'Honestly, Lou, you're his wife, not a hooker! Most women would be falling over themselves to spend his money. It's not like he can't afford to pay a few credit-card bills.'

'That's not the point,' said Lou stubbornly. 'Patrick's already been more than generous. We live for free in this fantastic house—the children even get to have their own pool!—and we don't do anything for him in return. It would be different if we were properly married.'

'Hey, I was your witness, remember?' said Marisa, unimpressed. 'It looked like a proper wedding to me. And you *can* do something for him now,' she pointed out. 'He's asked you to go and buy a posh frock, so let's go and find one to knock his socks off!'

They found it at the very end of the afternoon, just as Lou was ready to give up and go home.

'This is *it*!' Marisa held up a wonderful shimmering dress in that perfect shade of red between pink and scarlet. A layer of chiffon covered the arms and wafted over a simple silk under-dress. When Lou tried it on, the material slithered tantalisingly over her skin.

'She'll take it,' Marisa said to the sales assistant as soon as Lou stepped out of the changing room.

Lou was scandalised at the price, but Marisa overrode her, bullying her into matching sandals, earrings that glittered and swung tantalisingly, and an eye-catching bag, handmade with feathers and sequins.

'And you'll need a new lipstick too,' she said to Lou. 'I know just the colour.'

She insisted on coming round to supervise Lou's make-up on the night of the reception, too. 'You look fabulous!' she declared, standing back and eyeing her critically.

'You don't think it's a bit...much?' said Lou, who was rapidly losing her nerve. She felt ridiculously nervous, the way she had at sixteen before her first real date.

Which was stupid. This wasn't a date. She was just attending a function with her husband. Nothing to be nervous about in that.

It was just that this dress made her feel very aware of her own body. It made her feel...sexy. Too sexy for a forty-five-year-old who was supposed to be content with just being friends.

Patrick didn't help matters by looking devastatingly attractive in a dinner jacket whose severe black and white accentuated the hard lines of his face and sat easily on his powerful frame. He was waiting for her in the hall and Lou felt the breath leak out of her lungs as she walked down the stairs, very aware of the slippery material shifting suggestively over her body, and wishing that there were just a bit more chiffon to cover her cleavage.

'You look nice,' said Patrick in an odd voice.

Behind her, Lou heard Marisa let out a slow breath of exasperation. 'No, she doesn't look *nice*, Patrick. She looks absolutely gorgeous! Try that again,' she told him bossily, ignoring Lou's attempts to frown her down.

'You look gorgeous,' said Patrick obediently.

A chauffeured limousine was waiting for them outside, but Lou was too consumed by a mixture of disappointment and embarrassment to appreciate the luxury. She had wanted Patrick to think that she was gorgeous without prompting from Marisa, she realised. Now she felt as if she had tried too hard.

Beside her in the back of the car, Patrick was looking distant and preoccupied. Probably terrified that she was about to jump on him. Why on earth had she let Marisa bully her into this dress? Lou wondered desperately. She should have worn her old black silk trousers and cream top and been done with it.

It was a relief to get to the reception at last. It was a glittering affair, and the room seemed full of men looking far more distinguished than they merited in their dinner jackets, and beautiful women in fabulous dresses, many of them a lot more dramatic than Lou's. At least that meant that she looked less conspicuous. Less like a woman who had tried too hard to catch her husband's flagging attention.

She was agonisingly conscious of Patrick beside her, of his warm hand at her elbow as he introduced her, at the small of her back as he manoeuvred her through the crowd. Inevitably, they got separated after a while. Lou couldn't decide whether that made things easier or more difficult. She was quite capable of talking to people on her own, but even as she smiled and talked and listened she was acutely aware of Patrick a few yards away.

No sooner had she been detached from his side than one girl after another zeroed in on him. She could see them flirting openly with him, tilting their pretty heads appealingly, shaking back their blonde manes, laying their perfectly manicured hands on his sleeve, moving closer as they smiled suggestively.

Lou wanted to march over and slap their hands off him.

But she didn't have the right to do that. She had signed that away when she'd agreed to their pre-nuptial contract. She wasn't here to be jealous and possessive. She was only here to support Patrick and his business, and she had better not forget that.

Turning deliberately away from him, Lou smiled brilliantly at her companion, a young merchant banker called Charles who seemed visibly dazzled by her. It was nice to be appreciated for a change, Lou thought, her ego a little soothed. Nice to meet a man who didn't necessarily think that young blondes with long legs were the ultimate female company.

'I think we should go soon.' Patrick materialised at her elbow, looking grim.

'What, already?' Lou asked in surprise. They hadn't been there long.

'We've been here long enough,' he said.

Charles was looking a little daunted by the way Patrick was glaring at him, and Lou introduced the two men awkwardly, stumbling over describing Patrick as her husband.

Given no encouragement whatsoever to linger, Charles took himself off. 'I hope we'll meet again,' he said to Lou.

'I hope so too,' she said to make up for Patrick's rudeness. 'It was lovely to meet you. Really.'

'"*It was lovely to meet you*",' Patrick mimicked furiously as he propelled Lou towards the exit.

'Why were you so rude to him?' she demanded, practically running to keep up.

'I didn't like the way he was ogling you.'

Lou gaped at him. 'Ogling? He wasn't ogling me!'

'Come on, Lou, the guy was halfway down your dress!'

'At least he noticed me.' Lou's temper was simmering as she got into the car that was waiting for them at the bottom of the steps. 'It's more than you did. I might as well not have been there for all the notice you took of me.'

Patrick leant forward, had a word with the driver, and then closed the window between the front and back seats with a snap.

'Of course I noticed,' he said grittily. 'It was hard not to notice the way you were flirting.'

'I was not flirting,' said Lou through her teeth. 'I was being pleasant to your business associates, which is what you asked me to be.'

Patrick knew that. He had been watching her all evening out of the corner of his eye. She hadn't been the youngest woman there, or the best-dressed, or the prettiest, but she had the style and assurance of an older woman and an elusive charm that drew people to her. He just hadn't liked the way other men had looked at her in that dress.

Letting out a sigh, Patrick ran a hand through his hair. 'You're right, I'm sorry,' he said. 'You did a good job tonight. Lots of people told me how charming you were. You're obviously going to be a great asset to me. I'd rather you didn't wear that dress again, though,' he added, trying to sound humorous, but failing.

'Listen, you told me to go and buy a dress,' said Lou angrily. 'So I did. What's wrong with it?'

'There's nothing wrong with it. It's just that it's too...too...'

'Too *what*?'

'It's too disturbing,' Patrick said. 'It's the kind of dress that gives a man the wrong idea.'

And quite suddenly the atmosphere changed. Lou was stunned at how quickly she could go from anger and frustration to an electric awareness. The very air between them seemed to be vibrating as Patrick looked into her eyes, his deep, dark voice caressing her skin.

'It's the kind of dress that makes a man think about unzipping it,' he went on softly. 'It makes him think about what you're wearing underneath, what your skin would feel like...'

There didn't seem to be enough air to breathe properly. Unable to tear her eyes away from his, Lou moistened her lips. 'It wasn't meant to make you think that,' she managed.

'I know, but it does.' Tantalisingly, Patrick brushed the hair away from her face. 'That dress makes me wonder what it would be like to kiss you.'

'You should try wearing it,' said Lou unsteadily, desperately trying to make a joke of it. 'It makes you wonder more than that!'

'Does it now?' Patrick's smile gleamed in the darkness. 'Then maybe we should stop wondering and find out.'

A dim part of Lou's brain was jumping up and down and telling her that this was a bad idea—a *very* bad idea—but it was hard to pay attention to it when every nerve in her body was pointing out that this was what she had been thinking about for months.

She hadn't let herself accept the way her fingers itched to reach out and touch him whenever he sat near her. She hadn't wanted to admit how much she wanted to run her hands up his arms and over his shoulders so that she could feel the powerful flex of his muscles. How much she wanted to bury into his lean, hard body, to crawl all over him, to press her lips to his throat, to kiss the edges of his eyes, the corner of his mouth. How she wanted to feel him smile as she kissed him.

Or how much she wanted him to pull her into him, to roll her beneath him, to make love to her until they forgot everything but the clamour of their bodies.

And now, here, in the dim cocoon of this luxurious car, isolated from the outside world, she had her chance. *Go for it,* her body was yelling. *Don't listen to your brain!*

So Lou closed her mind and gave in to temptation. She didn't even hesitate as Patrick leant slowly towards her. Enveloped in hazy excitement, she lifted her hands to his shoulders and spread them over his back, revelling in the strength of his muscles beneath the dinner jacket, and as his mouth came down on hers she drew a breath of exquisite anticipation.

Giving herself up to the rush of pleasure, to the touch and taste of him, to his scent and his feel, she kissed him back with deep, hungry kisses. It felt wonderful to wrap her arms around his solid strength, to feel his hands slide over her, hot and insistent through the flimsy material of her dress, making her gasp with excitement, and she shivered at the press of his lips against her throat.

Her blood was pounding, her body booming so loudly that it took some time before she even realised that the car had stopped. 'We're home.' Patrick's ragged voice penetrated her swirling mind.

Home? Lou struggled to make sense of the word, struggled to remember where she was, what she was doing.

Somehow she found herself out on the gravel. Patrick was leaning through the front window, saying something to the driver, and then the car slid out of the drive and the gates closed silently behind it.

Patrick was still reeling from the rocketing excitement. How long had it been since he had necked in the back of a car like that? If the driver hadn't knocked to indicate that they had arrived just then...!

Smiling, he walked back to Lou, still standing exactly where he had left her and looking as shell-shocked as he felt. Who would have thought that a kiss could spin so quickly out of control?

'Your room or mine?' he said.

'Wait.' Lou put out her hands to ward him off as he reached for her. 'I'm not sure we should be doing this.'

'Not sure?' Patrick couldn't believe it. 'You seemed pretty sure in the back of the car there!'

'I know, I know.' She was trembling with reaction, but the air had cleared her head and she could think properly again.

'Don't try and tell me you don't want me,' he said angrily.

'No, I won't try and do that.' Lou swallowed. 'But you need to make a choice, Patrick. You can have me, or you can have your blondes, but you can't have both. I'm not going to sleep with you now and then accept that you have other girlfriends.'

'Lou...' Patrick raked his hands through his hair. 'Do we have to talk about this now?'

'Yes, we do,' she said. 'I need to know now whether

you want me enough to give up the freedom you said you wanted so much when we were married.'

Patrick stared at her. God, he wanted her. He had wanted her for months, he realised in a sudden moment of clarity. But give up his freedom? Tie himself down to commitment and fidelity, after one kiss? How could he decide that?

His hesitation told Lou everything she needed to know. 'Well, it looks like I've got my answer,' she said, and turned away to walk into the house. Alone.

CHAPTER NINE

LOU was weeding when Patrick got back from work the next evening. It was the first chance he'd had to talk to her alone since he'd been left standing angry and baffled on the gravel, and he'd been doing some thinking since then.

'I'm sorry about last night, Lou,' he said.

She leant back on her heels and looked at him. 'You don't need to apologise,' she said. 'It was as much my fault as yours. I got a bit carried away by that dress, that was all.'

'You were right to stop me when you did,' Patrick persevered. 'It would have been a mistake.' He hesitated. 'I want us to stay friends.'

'Of course,' she agreed instantly. 'I'd rather keep it that way too. Last night...it was just an itch that we both felt like scratching, but it would have complicated everything. Let's just forget it ever happened, shall we?' She mustered a smile. 'I won't wear the dress again!'

That would help, thought Patrick. He didn't think much of his chances of forgetting that kiss, though. Out loud, he said, 'I was thinking that I should go out more. See other women, the way I planned.'

Lou pulled a straggling weed out of her fork to hide the flash of dismay she felt. 'Good idea,' she said.

It *was* a good idea. She had come too close to getting hurt last night, and she wasn't risking that again. 'Have you got anyone in mind?'

'Well, yes,' said Patrick awkwardly.

He had found the card the young lawyer had slipped him

at the reception in his jacket pocket that morning. Fingering it, he remembered her vaguely. Tall, blonde, very attractive, very assured. The card said that her name was Holly. Patrick didn't remember that. All he remembered was how uncomfortable he had felt at her open interest. She must have been able to see his wedding ring. He had only taken the card because it had been less trouble than refusing it.

Holly wasn't quite his usual type, but she was obviously intelligent, beautiful, and ambitious. She hadn't struck him as a woman who would be much bothered with emotional commitment, or the fact that he was married. After a sleepless night trying to convince himself that he had made the right decision in choosing his freedom over Lou, Patrick thought that Holly might be just the kind of woman he needed right then.

'Great.' Lou gave him a brilliant smile, determined to show him that she would be sticking to her side of the deal from now on. 'Is she nice?'

'She seems nice,' said Patrick, but he couldn't help remembering what Lou had said about wanting a relationship with someone prepared to sleep with a married man. 'Her name's Holly,' he blurted out, pushing the memory aside.

'Pretty name,' said Lou, attacking a rogue dandelion.

Her dark head was bent and Patrick watched her, wishing that he knew what she was thinking. 'I thought I'd take her to dinner,' he said. 'Are you OK with that?'

'Of course.' Lou shook back her hair and smiled again as she tossed the dandelion onto the pile of weeds. 'It's what we agreed, isn't it? Don't worry about me. I'm more than happy with the way things have worked out, Patrick. We made a deal and I'm happy to stick to it. You go. Enjoy yourself.'

He didn't, of course. Holly was smart, attractive, successful and clearly up for a no-strings relationship. Exactly the kind of woman Patrick had had in mind when he'd first made his deal with Lou. She had no intention of settling down until she had made a name for herself. Holly was going far, and she couldn't be bothered with emotional entanglements that might slow her down.

He should have dated women like her before, Patrick told himself, but the more Holly talked about her need for independence, the more he caught echoes of things he had said himself in the past, and he shifted uncomfortably. There was a ruthless quality to her, an utter lack of sentiment or any real warmth that appalled him. Was that how *he* seemed to other people?

He took Holly to the latest restaurant, where she picked at the wonderful food and he thought about Lou. She would have eaten with the kids. Patrick wondered how Grace had got on with her maths test while Holly talked about the glittering career she had mapped out for herself. Tom had been playing in a football match that afternoon, he remembered. Lou had gone to watch him. Patrick would have liked to have gone with her.

The evening seemed endless. He drove Holly back to her trendy apartment, but made an excuse when she invited him up for a nightcap. He wanted to go home.

Lou was already in bed when he got in, but she had left some lights on for him. Patrick wandered through the house, noticing how much warmer and more welcoming it was these days. The kitchen table was covered with school books. He picked up Tom's French exercise book and grinned at the excruciating errors. Tom was a mechanic, not a linguist.

There was a jug of flowers on the window sill, and the kitchen smelled appetising. Patrick sniffed. They must have had something cheesy for supper. He wished he had been there instead of eating his way through the elaborate and expensive meal he had shared with Holly.

He walked softly upstairs. Lou's door was closed. Hesitating outside it, Patrick wished that he could go in and sit on the edge of her bed. They could talk the way they had used to talk and he could tell her about his awful evening and the feeling he had that he had got everything very wrong.

But he couldn't do that, not after last night. He had made his choice, and now he would have to stick with it.

'Mum, can we go away at half-term?'

Lou was wrapping sandwiches in cling film and trying not to be too aware of Patrick, reading the *Financial Times* at the end of the kitchen table.

The atmosphere between them had been strained ever since he had started dating Holly. Lou didn't know what he saw in the woman, but the relationship certainly didn't seem to be making him particularly happy. He was brusque and irritable a lot of the time, rather the way he had been when she'd first met him, Lou thought. It made it difficult to maintain the friendship that had been so easy that summer.

It was partly her fault, Lou knew. She was trying to be pleasant about it, but the effort of appearing not to mind that he was seeing another woman had left her tense and the only way she could cope was to withdraw into herself. She was spending a lot of time in the garden these days, but it wasn't having the same restorative effect it used to have. She was snappy with the kids, too, which wasn't fair on them, and the guilt only made her worse.

'I thought we'd go and see Fenny,' she told Grace, packing the sandwiches neatly into their lunchboxes. 'We haven't seen her since the wedding.'

'Oh, Mu-um...' Grace moaned. 'Not Yorkshire *again*!'

'Yes, can't we go somewhere different?' Tom chimed in between mouthfuls of cereal.

Lou kept her voice even with difficulty. 'You love Fenny,' she reminded them.

'Yes, but she could come here, couldn't she?' said Grace. 'We don't have to spend a whole week there. It's so *boring*.'

Lou thought of the green hills and the river, of walking in the wind and the rain and coming in to a roaring fire and Fenny's scones. Of clean air and simple needs and no Patrick twisting her entrails into knots and making it hard to breathe. No trying to convince herself that she had been right to walk away from him that night, that it was better to just be friends. Suddenly she yearned to be there.

'It's not boring, Grace,' she said tightly. 'If you're bored there, that's your problem, not Yorkshire's.'

Grace looked mutinous. 'India's going to Majorca. And Marina's dad says he'll take her to New York!'

'You've got a dad, too,' said Lou with an edge to her voice. She found two apples in the fruit bowl and polished them on her sleeve before wedging them in next to the sandwiches. 'Ask him to take you.'

'I did, and he said it would be better if we went with you.'

That sounded like Lawrie, thought Lou bitterly.

'He said you could afford it more than him now,' Tom offered helpfully.

Lou sucked in her breath and bit back an angry rejoinder. She tried so hard not to criticise Lawrie in front of the children, but when she thought about the money he must have spent on his new sports car, a fraction of which would have enabled him to take Grace and Tom on the holiday they craved, she wanted to scream and shout and hit something.

She vented her fury on the lunchboxes instead, slamming them both shut.

'I'm sorry, but I've already told Fenny we'd go and see her.'

The children immediately set up a chorus of moans. 'It's not *fair*!'

'If you're not careful, we won't go anywhere,' she said, warning in her voice. 'It's not as if you'd miss out on much. You've got your own pool here, for heaven's sake! What else do you need?'

Tom and Grace exchanged martyred looks. 'It's not the same as going away,' Tom said. 'And you *can* afford it, Mum. I mean, that's why you married Patrick, isn't it?'

Sensing that Lou was at the end of her tether, Patrick put down his newspaper. 'That's enough,' he said sternly.

'But, Patrick, you want to go away somewhere, don't you?' Grace tried to cajole him.

'Patrick has a job to do,' said Lou quickly, not wanting him to get any more involved. 'He'll probably be busy at the end of October.'

And there was always Holly to keep him at home now.

'I could probably take some time off,' said Patrick. He glanced at Lou, who was at the sink, the set of her shoulders tense. She hadn't said anything to him about half-term, he realised. Perhaps she didn't want him to go with them?

'Lou?' he said tentatively. 'Maybe we can work something out here.'

She turned, wiping her hands on a tea towel. 'What sort of something?'

'Why don't you go and see Fenny on your own? There's no reason why you shouldn't go next week if you want.

I'll look after the kids. And then perhaps we could all go away together at half-term?'

'Oh, yes! Yes! *Please*!' Grace and Tom were ecstatic, but Patrick held up a hand to check their exuberance.

'I want to know what your mother thinks first.'

Lou was torn. Part of her longed to go away on her own, but there had been nothing in their agreement about Patrick looking after the children. He hadn't wanted anything to do with them at all, but now he was offering, not only to care for them, but also take them away for a week for a holiday she was pretty sure he wouldn't enjoy.

'That seems to be asking a lot of you,' she prevaricated.

'Not really.' He shrugged. 'I'm quite happy to do that. I just don't want to undermine your authority. If you think Grace and Tom should go to Yorkshire with you at half-term, then that's what will happen, and there'll be no more arguing. I was simply suggesting a compromise.'

He was offering her a way out of what would otherwise turn into an entrenched battle of wills, Lou realised. This was not the time to stand on her dignity. That would just make things worse.

'It sounds a good compromise to me,' she said.

Grace and Tom were delighted and immediately set up a clamour of conflicting demands about the holiday.

'OK, here's the deal,' said Patrick, shouting them down at last. 'You two go away and agree on the kind of holiday you want. You choose a country that's within three hours' flying time from London, and what you want to do when you're there, and we'll all go there for a week.'

'We can *choose*?' They couldn't believe their luck.

'Only if you stop hassling your mother,' he warned them, and they nodded eagerly as they scrambled off their chairs and gathered up their school bags.

'OK, Patrick.'

'That was very kind of you,' Lou said quietly when they had gone.

Patrick made a big deal of folding up his newspaper. 'Anything for a quiet life,' he said.

'Still…'

He looked up and their eyes met for what seemed the first time in weeks. 'You look tired,' he said roughly, not liking the drawn look she had.

'I haven't been sleeping well recently,' she admitted. 'I don't know why.'

Although it probably had a lot to do with the fact that he was seeing another woman and she was supposed not to care.

'You could probably do with a break,' said Patrick, and the warm concern in his eyes made her want to cry.

'It sounds wonderful,' she admitted. 'But I don't feel I deserve it. It's not as if I have a hard life here.'

'Go and have a holiday anyway. I expect Fenny would like to see you on your own.'

'But I can't leave the kids,' she said, fighting temptation. 'Someone really has to be here when they get in from school.'

'I can do that for a few days. I've got a computer here. There's plenty I can do from home if I need to.'

'What about meals, though?' Lou fretted and Patrick pushed back his chair.

'I'm not entirely helpless. I can peel a potato and use a microwave. They won't get the kind of meals you cook for them, but it won't kill them for a few days. We'll manage.'

Lou thought Tom and Grace would probably love a week of not being made to eat fresh fruit and vegetables the whole time.

'What about Holly?' she blurted out and Patrick stilled for a moment as he shrugged on his jacket.

He had taken Holly out once more. They had gone to the opera one night, but the evening hadn't been any more of a success than the first one, and he had found himself repelled by her ruthlessness and unconcern about the fact that he was married. When he had made another excuse to leave her at her door, she had laughed mockingly.

'Funny, I didn't have you down as the hen-pecked type. Is she very fierce, your wife?'

Patrick was furious that Holly would dare mention Lou. 'She's worth a thousand of you,' he said coldly.

Holly smiled with calculated allure and stepped closer to run a suggestive hand down his lapel. 'Then why are you here?'

Patrick detached her hand with distaste. 'I don't know,' he said.

Now he looked across at Lou, still sitting at the kitchen table with tired eyes and a worried expression. She would look washed out next to Holly today. Holly was cleverer, smarter, prettier.

And Lou was warmer and kinder and more loving.

'You don't need to worry about Holly,' he told her.

Lou left for Yorkshire two days later. Patrick missed her horribly. He kept looking for her, expecting to turn round and see her, dark and warm. He felt restless and uneasy, forever fidgeting and unable to concentrate on work. It was as if he were waiting and waiting for something, but he didn't know what it was.

Whatever it was, he wished it would just hurry up. He hated feeling like this. Patrick was proud of his ability to focus. It was the secret of his success, after all. Always he had been able to identify what he wanted, and go for it.

Now he didn't even know what he wanted.

Unless it was for Lou to come home.

The house was empty without her, even though Grace and Tom were there. They seemed to accept their mother's absence more readily than he did, and were full of plans for the half-term holiday, heatedly arguing over which resort was likely to have the most attractions for them.

Patrick made sure they rang Lou every night. He thought she would want to hear from them, but deep down he knew his reminders were purely selfish. He could always think of an excuse to take the phone when the kids had finished and hear her voice.

She was having a great time, she told him. She and Fenny pottered around the garden, and she had been for some long walks on her own. She felt much better. The weather was beautiful. If it weren't for the kids, she would be tempted to stay for ever.

'I think they'd miss you,' said Patrick. *I'd miss you.*

'They sound absolutely fine,' said Lou, and he could hear the smile in her voice. 'But I supposed I'd better come home and let you get back to work. I'll see you on Friday.'

Patrick couldn't wait. He caught himself looking at the clock and calculating how many hours until he would see her. Pathetic. He rolled his eyes at himself. Anyone would think he was in love with her.

Anyone would think he was in love with her.

He rewound mentally and played the same thought over more slowly while the truth of it sank into his mind. Of course anyone would think that. They would think it because it was true. He was in love with Lou.

How had *that* happened?

Falling in love with Lou hadn't been the idea at all. Patrick sat stunned at his own obtuseness. Oh, he could appreciate the irony. After all those years avoiding love, avoiding commitment, running away from the beautiful girls who tried to get too close, it turned out that the only woman he wanted was a middle-aged mother of two.

A middle-aged mother who had insensibly become the centre of his existence, whose dark eyes lit with laughter, and whose presence calmed and consoled him in a way nothing else could.

A middle-aged mother who only wanted to be his friend.

I'll never fall in love again, she had said. Lawrie had hurt her too much, she had said. She didn't want to love again. It would take a lot for her to trust enough to love him the way he loved her, Patrick realised, especially given the deal they had made.

So he wouldn't tell her yet. He would try first to get back the easy friendship they had lost since that kiss in the back of the limousine. They had both been trying since then, but it hadn't been the same, and they both knew it. That could change, though. And when they were friends again, he would tell her that he didn't want his precious freedom any more. He only wanted her.

Lou was his wife, after all. Surely he could tell her that?

Together with Grace and Tom, Patrick planned a special meal to welcome Lou back that Friday. Most of it was pre-prepared, it was true, but they had chosen each dish carefully, laid the table and lit candles.

'We even got salad for you, Mum,' said Tom, wanting to make sure that she appreciated the lengths they had gone to for her.

Lou looked at the three of them and her throat felt so tight she was afraid she might cry. 'It all looks lovely. Thank you.'

'We missed you,' Grace said. 'Didn't we, Patrick?'

'Yes, we did.' Patrick was amazed at how calm his voice sounded. Inside he felt like a stammering schoolboy. His chest hurt at the sight of her smile, and he was so pleased to see her again he could hardly speak.

Lou was glad to be home. She had enjoyed her time with Fenny, and was restored by her week away. She had been doing a lot of thinking on her long walks in the hills, and she knew now how close she had come to falling in love with Patrick.

Patrick had never pretended that he loved her, or that there was any chance of him loving her. She had been a fool to forget how much it had hurt when she'd realised that Lawrie didn't love her any more. Her world had fallen apart, and she wasn't going to let herself get hurt like that again. The dull ache she had felt when he had told her about Holly was a mere foretaste of what would be to come, and Lou couldn't face it.

She hadn't fallen too far, she convinced herself. She could stop now, seal off her heart, and not let herself feel any more for him than tepid friendship. It was merely a matter of mind over matter as in the old calypso song that her mother used to play.

And so it was. Lou didn't think it would be easy, but she knew she could do it. Living with Patrick would complicate matters, but she couldn't leave him. Grace and Tom were so happy. They didn't just accept Patrick, they liked him, and he liked them. Lou wouldn't do anything to jeopardise that relationship. Her children had had enough upheaval in their lives.

But she had to protect herself, too, so she would go back and be a friend to Patrick, just as she had promised. No more lying awake when he was out, wondering what he and Holly were doing. No more yearning for the impossible. No more would her heart pound when he walked into the room, Lou vowed to herself. She wouldn't even *think* about touching him, holding him, kissing him.

That way lay heartache, and her heart was scarred enough as it was.

'I'm sorry I was so tense before I went away,' she told Patrick that night after Grace and Tom had gone to bed.

'You seem much more relaxed now,' he commented, thinking how much better the world seemed just because she was there on the other side of the table.

'I am,' she said. 'I've been doing a lot of thinking.'

'What about?'

'About us. About our marriage.'

'Oh?' Patrick's guts knotted in anticipation. Was it possible that she had changed her mind too?

'I've realised how important our friendship is to me,' said Lou. 'I think I was a little jealous of Holly,' she admitted honestly, 'but I know that being friends is worth so much more than a physical relationship. I just wanted you to know that I won't be tense like that again when you go out with her or anyone else for that matter. That sidc of your life is nothing to do with me, and I want it to stay that way.'

Right, so no change of mind, then. Patrick fought down the disappointment. 'Great,' he said.

Lou got up and smiled at him. 'I don't think I've ever thanked you properly for everything you've done for us, Patrick,' she said. 'You've given us somewhere wonderful to live. The children are happy. Thanks to you, Fenny and I had a lovely week together.' She gestured at the guttering candles. 'And now this lovely meal.'

Sitting heavily in his chair, Patrick closed his eyes and breathed in the scent of her perfume as she bent and kissed him on the cheek, very gently. 'Thank you,' she said softly. 'This is the only way I'll kiss you now, so you don't need to worry about any more emotional hassles. I'm glad we didn't make love that night. It's better to be dear friends, isn't it?'

What could he say? 'Yes,' said Patrick in a curiously colourless voice. 'Much better.'

'So how are things going with you and Patrick?' Marisa asked a few weeks later. She was sitting at the kitchen table, filing her nails while Lou got supper ready. They were going out for an evening together as soon as Patrick got home.

'Fine,' said Lou. 'Great, in fact.'

They *were* great, she thought. Grace and Tom's choice of Minorca for a holiday had been a great success, and Patrick had joined in with everything with good grace. Back home, he didn't seem to be going out very much at all so that they had almost got their old, easy companionship back.

Almost, but not quite. Not once, by a word or a look, did Patrick ever do anything to suggest that he wanted more than quiet friendship either. Sometimes Lou even wondered if she had dreamt that wild, passionate kiss they had shared. In the circumstances, she should have been able to relax completely, but she still didn't seem to be able to do anything about the instinctive tightening of her muscles at the sight of him, or about the subtle shift in the atmosphere when he was in the room.

Mind over matter, Lou reminded herself when she found herself noticing it too much.

'Still on the just-good-friends thing?' asked Marisa, apparently intent on a hangnail.

'Yes.' Lou could hear the faintly defensive note in her voice. 'Why?'

'I just wondered. I saw your face when Patrick came in the other day, that's all.'

'What day was that?'

'You know, Grace's birthday.'

'Oh, then.' Lou rummaged in the fridge to avoid Marisa's sharp eyes. For all her friend only ever seemed to be concerned about her appearance, she missed nothing.

Patrick had come back from work on that wet November evening to find the kitchen full of warmth and light and laughter. Grace had invited her three closest friends round, and they had lobbied to make pancakes in lieu of a more traditional birthday dinner. There had been flour everywhere and stray splatters of pancake batter had decorated the work surfaces.

Lou had been supervising. Marisa, there in her role as Grace's godmother, had been drinking champagne and keeping well out of the range of the pancake tossing, but Tom had been in the thick of it and allowed to have his own go at flipping a pancake in the air.

There had been much giggling when Patrick had walked in.

'Patrick, come and have a go,' Grace insisted, dragging him over to the table.

'Give him a chance to get his coat off, Grace,' Lou protested, but she might as well have saved her breath. Patrick was bullied into discarding his jacket and rolling up his sleeves.

'I've never done this before,' he said as he loosened his tie.

'It's quite difficult,' Tom told him. 'Mum can do it, but the rest of us are useless.'

'I did it,' Grace fired up immediately. 'Sort of. But you show him, Mum,' she added graciously.

So Lou showed Patrick how to pour in the batter and swirl it round, then wait for just the right moment before giving the pan a quick, sharp flip.

She was standing very close to him, close enough to smell the clean, distinctive male scent of him. Close enough to see the texture of his skin, the way his hair grew, and the prickle of stubble on his jaw. Close enough to count the lines starring his eyes. It was hard to breathe there for a minute. Hard to remember that it was merely a matter of mind over matter.

Patrick made a comical face and flipped the pancake over, just catching it back in the pan. He turned with a mock bow to receive the applause of his audience.

'You did it!' The children were all gratifyingly impressed.

'Beginner's luck,' Patrick explained over the excitement and glanced at Lou with a smile. 'And a good teacher!'

He had given Grace shaggy snow boots for her birthday. They were for her to take on the skiing trip she had so longed for and which was now confirmed. Lou remembered how Grace's face had lit up that morning when she'd opened them, the easy way she'd hugged Patrick to thank him.

She watched him laughing with the children as they insisted that he eat the pancake he had tossed so impressively. Grace sprinkled on sugar while Tom leant against Patrick's shoulder, and Lou's heart contracted at the sight of them together.

And of course Marisa had seen.

'How long are you going to keep up this pretence that you don't love him?' said Marisa, holding the back of her hand up to inspect her nails.

There was a tiny pause. 'I don't love him,' said Lou.

Marisa sighed. 'Lou. Look at me.' Reluctantly Lou met her friend's eyes. 'Now say that again.'

'I don't *want* to love him,' Lou said wretchedly, abandoning the supper to slump down at the table opposite her friend. 'I want things to stay as they are. I want us to be friends.' If she said it enough, she would believe it.

'Friends isn't enough when you look at a man the way you look at Patrick,' said Marisa.

'It's better than being hurt.'

'Lou, Patrick isn't Lawrie. I'm sure he's stubborn and pigheaded and unbelievably difficult a lot of the time, but basically he's a good man. And he loves you.'

'He doesn't.'

'Of course he does.' Marisa rolled her eyes. 'God, it's so obvious! Honestly, Lou, I can't believe you two are being so obtuse. The man can't take his eyes off you.'

'Really?' Lou was torn between disbelief and hope.

'Yes, *really*, and it's time you did something about it. You're married to a good man who you love and who loves you. Why are you wasting time like this?'

Lou chewed her thumb. 'I don't want to risk what we've got,' she tried to explain.

'Then you're a fool,' said Marisa roundly. 'Sure, it's good to be friends, but you've got other friends. You could have Patrick as a lover as well. You could have a real marriage.'

She gave an exasperated sigh when Lou still dithered uncertainly. 'You've talked a lot over the years about wanting Grace and Tom to grow up with the example of a loving relationship, Lou. Well, give them one! Don't waste your life being afraid that he'll let you down and hurt you the way Lawrie did. There are no guarantees in any relationship, and I guess you'll have to work at it, but it seems to me that a strong and loving marriage would be worth the effort and the risk.'

It would be. Of course it would be. But only if Patrick wanted it too, and Lou wasn't sure that he did. He had chosen his freedom over her once before.

She tried to explain this to Marisa. 'And I've spent so long insisting that I just want to be friends, I wouldn't know how to tell him that I've changed my mind.'

'You could always try sending the kids to bed early and coming down in stockings, high heels and something lacy,' said Marisa. 'He'd be bound to get the point then.'

'I can't do that!' Lou felt her face grow hot at the very thought. 'It would just embarrass Patrick.'

Marisa grinned. 'It's a long time since you've been with a man, isn't it, Lou? Of *course* he wouldn't be embarrassed. He'd be too busy not being able to believe his luck! And Patrick looks like a stocking man to me. I saw the way he was looking at that suit you wore at the wedding.'

'I'm not prancing around in stockings!'

'Well, then, you're going to have to fall back on the last resort of relationships in crisis.'

'What's that?'

'Talking,' said Marisa. 'I hate to break it to you, Lou, but you're both big people. For heaven's sake, just sit him down and tell him how you feel!'

Easy for Marisa to say, thought Lou the following evening as she waited edgily for the time when she could legitimately send Grace and Tom to bed. By the time she and Patrick were finally alone, she was in such a dither that she could hardly sit still.

'I was, er, wondering if we could have a little chat,' she said and grimaced inwardly as she heard herself. She sounded as if she were inviting the office junior in to talk about unpunctuality.

'Sure.' Patrick looked a little surprised at her formal tone. 'Is this serious?'

'No…well, yes…in a way…' Lou trailed off helplessly.

'Shall we have a drink, then?'

'Good idea.' She certainly needed one.

When Patrick brought her a whisky, she gulped at it for courage. After a moment's hesitation, he sat down at the other end of the cream sofa.

'What is it, Lou?'

Lou cleared her throat. 'Well, I was just wondering…that is…well, no, the thing is…' Oh, God, how *were* you supposed to ask your husband to make love to you?

She was still dithering about how to put it, and beginning to wonder if it might not have been easier to go for the stocking option after all, when the phone rang.

It was the perfect diversion. Lou leapt up to answer it, but as she listened to the voice at the other end the colour drained slowly from her face.

'Lou?' Patrick got up in concern as she put the phone down and he saw her expression. 'What is it?'

'It's Fenny,' she said in a voice that seemed to belong to someone else entirely. 'She's had a stroke.'

CHAPTER TEN

LOU wanted to set off immediately. 'I've got to get to the hospital,' she said, pacing around the room, desperately trying to work out what needed to be done. 'If I got a taxi to the station, I might still be able to get a train... I'll have to tell the kids... Perhaps I should take them with me, but it's too late to wake them up...'

Chewing her thumb anxiously, she turned to Patrick. 'What do you think?'

'I think you should sit down and drink this,' said Patrick, topping up her glass of whisky. 'You're not going anywhere tonight.'

'But I must see Fenny!' she protested as he pushed her gently back onto the sofa and made sure that her fingers had closed around the glass.

'There's nothing you can do tonight, Lou. Even if you get the last train north, you won't be able to get a connection to Skipton. We'll get up early tomorrow morning and I'll drive you to the hospital. If we leave at five, we could be there by nine.'

'But you've got meetings...'

He shrugged. 'Meetings can be rearranged.'

Lou felt shaky and close to tears. 'What about Grace and Tom?'

'We'll ring Marisa in a minute. She'll come and look after things here.' Patrick sat down next to Lou and nodded at the whisky. 'Drink that. It'll steady you.'

Obediently, Lou took a sip, choking a little as the fiery liquid hit the back of her throat.

'Better?'

The peaty warmth was spreading down her throat and settling in her stomach, and Lou felt steadier, just as he had said she would.

'Yes. Sorry. I don't seem to be able to think clearly.'

'You don't need to think about anything right now.' He took her hand. 'I'll sort it out. Now, tell me what Fenny's neighbour said.'

His warm, firm clasp was immensely comforting, but made it harder to be strong. Tears prickled behind Lou's eyes and she blinked them fiercely back.

'She didn't know much. She'd just popped in to see Fenny about flowers for the church, and she found her lying on the kitchen floor. She called an ambulance, and went with them to the hospital because there wasn't anyone else.' Lou drew a shaky breath. 'She told me the doctors said it wasn't looking good.'

She looked at Patrick, her dark eyes stark. 'Fenny's my rock,' she said, trying to keep her voice under control, but it cracked a little all the same. 'I can't bear to lose her. It would be like losing my mother all over again.'

'I know,' he said, and his grip tightened around her hand. 'I know.'

With a huge effort, Lou pulled herself together. She put down her whisky and dabbed her fingers under her eyes to stop any rogue tears from spilling over. 'I mustn't carry on like this,' she said. 'I've got to be strong.'

Patrick let go of her hand and pulled her firmly into his arms. It wasn't the way he had wanted to be holding her, but right now she needed to be held like a child, not a woman, and after a moment's resistance he felt her weaken and turn instinctively into him.

'You don't need to be strong tonight,' he said, resting his cheek against her silky hair. 'I'm here.'

* * *

Fenny looked very small and very frail in the hospital bed. She had always been so active that Lou had never thought of her as elderly, but she looked old now. Throat tight, Lou sat beside her aunt and held her thin hand, willing her to get better.

But Fenny didn't get better. At one point she opened her eyes and saw Lou sitting desperately beside her.

'…oo,' she slurred.

'Yes, Fenny, it's me, Lou. I'm here.'

Fenny tried to say something else, and Lou leant forward to try and make out the word.

'Patrick?' she guessed, and Fenny managed a tiny nod of assent.

'Patrick's with me. He's just outside. Look, here he is,' she said, turning as she heard the door open behind her.

Patrick moved over to the bed so Fenny could see him. He had been talking to the ward sister who had told him that Fenny was sinking fast. 'Hello, Fenny,' he said, and his voice was so normal, so reassuring, that Lou wanted to cry all over again. Funny how he could make everything seem better just by standing there.

Fenny struggled to say something more, her eyes trying to convey some urgent message as they flicked between him and Lou, and Patrick suddenly realised what it was that she wanted.

He put a hand on Lou's shoulder. 'Don't worry, Fenny,' he said. 'I'll look after Lou. I promise.'

There was no mistaking the relief in Fenny's eyes, and one side of her mouth tried to smile. '-ood,' she said, and visibly relaxed, lapsing back into sleep.

She died just over an hour later, very quietly, with Lou still holding her hand.

Patrick dealt with everything. He talked to the nurses and

made all the arrangements, while Lou sat numbly, unable to take in the fact that Fenny had gone. Then he put his hand under her elbow and guided her out of the hospital, and put her in the car. He didn't try to make her talk. He just made sure the car was warm, and drove her back to Fenny's house, where he lit the fire and made her tea, and then held her when the numbness cracked and she fell apart.

He let her cry until she was too exhausted to cry any more, and then he took her upstairs and put her in a chair while he made the bed up for her. Numb with misery, pig-eyed from crying, Lou sat unresisting as he wiped her face with a flannel and helped her out of her clothes.

For the next couple of days, he was everywhere, dealing with all the practicalities, gently bullying Lou into eating, buttoning her coat and taking her out for a blustery walk, cleaning the fire and laying it so that he could light it for her as soon as she came in.

And gradually, Lou began to feel better, better enough to feel a real pang when Patrick told her that he was going back to London.

'I'll go and get Grace and Tom,' he said. 'They'd want to be here for the funeral. We'll be back tomorrow.' He hesitated, looking at Lou in concern. 'Will you be OK here on your own for a night?'

'Yes, I'll be fine,' said Lou. 'I'm OK now.'

But she missed him horribly when he had gone.

I'm relying on him, she thought, watching the Porsche drive out of sight, and letting her hand fall forlornly to her side. It was so long since she had let herself rely on anyone that it felt strange. Strange and indescribably comforting.

They buried Fenny on a crisp winter day. The trees were stark against a pale blue sky and the bite in the air brought colour to Grace's pale cheeks. Lou held her hand, and

Patrick stood beside her, a comforting hand on Tom's shoulder.

Lou watched desolately as Fenny's coffin was lowered into the ground next to her husband. Fenny had been there for her when her parents died, when Lawrie left her, through all the bad times, and the good. And she had understood what it was like to be on your own. A widow for thirty-five years, she had only been forty-nine when Donald had died.

Not much older than Lou was now. Lou felt sick and giddy at the thought. How would she feel if she lost Patrick? If she had to spend thirty-five years wishing that she had made the most of the time they had together, as Fenny and Donald had done, instead of pretending that she didn't care, that it didn't matter if Patrick didn't love her the way she loved him?

She glanced at Patrick, standing massive and reassuring beside her, offering her son unobtrusive comfort, and she remembered how anxious Fenny had been to see him, how her aunt had relaxed at his promise. *I'll look after Lou,* he had said.

Surely he loved her too? Like Fenny, he had been there when she'd needed him. For the first time, Lou hadn't had to deal with everything by herself. Patrick had done it all. He wouldn't have done that unless he loved her, would he?

The only question was *how* he loved her. Did he love her as a dear friend, or as a wife?

She was going to have to find out, Lou resolved. Not right then, when they were all still so upset about Fenny, but soon. Marisa was right. Their marriage couldn't carry on the way it had been. Being friends wasn't enough, and Lou was just going to have to do something about it.

Patrick drove Grace and Tom back to London the next day. Lou was going to stay on for a few more days to sort out Fenny's things and see her solicitor about settling her affairs, but the children needed to go back to school, and Patrick had some urgent meetings he couldn't put off any longer.

'I'll come and get you next weekend,' he said to Lou as he closed the boot of the car. She had kissed Grace and Tom goodbye, and stood waiting to wave them off, hugging her arms against the cold.

'You know, there's no need for you to drive up and down the country like this,' she tried. 'I could get the train back.'

Patrick opened the driver's door. 'I'll be back on Friday night,' he said as if she hadn't spoken.

As she had known he would. She was getting used to being looked after, Lou thought guiltily. But it was a nice feeling.

'Thank you for everything, Patrick,' she said.

He hesitated, then came back and kissed her on the cheek. 'Take care,' he said

A peck on the cheek, was it? That was going to change.

'Drive carefully,' said Lou, and gave him a friendly hug in return. She could do friends. For now.

What she needed was a plan of action. Lou waved until the car was out of sight, and then turned back to go into the cottage. Inside, the fire was swept and laid ready for her to light it. Patrick must have done that this morning while she was having a bath.

She searched for the matches on the mantelpiece. Crouching in front of the fire, she struck a match and held it out to a piece of paper, watching as the flame caught, flickered and then grew, spreading under the kindling.

Like her feelings for Patrick, really. It was hard to remember now how completely uninterested she had been in him when she had first met him. Three months working with him, and not once had she noticed his mouth or his hands or the way his eyes lit when he smiled. Not a flicker.

Then there had been that night in Newcastle. That had been a spark.

And then that kiss in the back of the car. That had been a definite flicker.

Now Lou wanted a blaze.

Patrick had been so kind over the last few days. She thought about that first night when they had come back from the hospital to find the cottage empty. His kindness and gentleness had been what she'd needed that night, but she didn't need that any more. She wanted him to take her to bed again, and this time she wanted him to treat her like a woman, not a friend. She wanted him to be demanding, not gentle, hot, not warm, but he wouldn't be as long as they stuck to their agreement to be just friends.

Their marriage was just like the fire that Patrick had made for her so carefully that morning, thought Lou. It had everything necessary to burn but right now it was cold, still perfectly laid, needing only a match to get it going.

And she would light it when Patrick came back.

Patrick parked the car outside the cottage. It was late, but he hadn't wanted to wait another day before seeing Lou. The lights were on in the house, glowing and welcoming through the dark and the rain.

The next moment the front door opened and Lou appeared, silhouetted in a rectangle of yellow light. Patrick felt the tension inside him release at the sight of her. It had been a wet and windy drive, with endless hold-ups on the motorway as the heavy traffic crept along nose to tail, but it was worth it to think that he would be walking into the warm house and she would be there, smiling.

He was going to tell her how he felt. Patrick had decided

that on the way up in the car. He wasn't that sure if this was the right time—it wasn't that long since Fenny had died, after all—but he wasn't going to ask anything of Lou or make any demands. He would give her all the time she wanted. He just needed to say that he loved her, that was all.

Pulling his mac over his head, he grabbed his overnight bag and ran through the rain for the door.

'Hello.' Lou stepped back to let him into the warm, and Patrick was seized by an inexplicable shyness as he shook the raindrops from his coat. What was going on? He had never been shy in his life. It was just Lou. His wife.

She looked so beautiful, though, with her dark eyes and her dark hair. She was wearing a soft red jumper and a straight skirt that stopped at her knees and reminded him irresistibly of those little suits she had worn when she was his PA, the ones that she might or might not have been wearing stockings with. Just looking at her made Patrick's chest hurt.

But there was a constraint about her that made him hesitate. It wasn't shyness, he realised. It was fear that she might not want him the way he so desperately wanted her. He would have to be very careful.

'Let me take that for you.' Lou took his coat and hung it up on a hook.

She was nervous. She had thought it all through, and now she had a plan. Even if they hadn't been interrupted by that awful phone call from Fenny's neighbour, Lou knew that she would have made a mess of sitting down and talking to him. It had been too difficult to find the right words.

So now she was going to try Marisa's first suggestion. She was going to seduce her own husband.

All she needed to do, Lou had decided, was to build up

some sexual tension, the kind that had fizzled so unexpectedly across the restaurant table in Newcastle. Then it would be a question of not spooking him. She needed to be sexy, but subtle. She had already created an intimate atmosphere in the sitting room, with the sofa pulled up in front of the fire, and a single table lamp adding a soft glow to the flickering firelight.

The only problem was her outfit. She didn't have anything remotely sexy in the clothes department with her. Understandably, it had been the last thing on her mind when she had thrown a few things into a case that night she had heard about Fenny's stroke. This jumper and skirt were the best she could do. Not exactly the slinky, shimmery little number that would slide off her shoulders at the mere brush of his fingers.

Still, slinky, silky dresses weren't ideal for opening the door on a night like this, or for hanging around in cold Dales kitchens, and she would probably have ruined the whole effect by putting a cardigan on whenever she left the warmth of the fire.

Once there, though, it would be fine. She would sit next to him on the sofa and inch gradually closer. She would run her fingers through her hair, make a lot of eye contact, moisten her lips a lot. She had seen it on television and it always worked then.

And then—Lou was a bit hazy about how this would happen exactly—they would kiss, and whoosh! The match would start the fire.

It was a good plan, but her desired image as a sultry, mysterious seductress was immediately thrown off balance when Patrick filled the hall, his nearness making her woozy, making it hard to remember her careful plan, urging her instead just to jump him and tell him she'd die if he didn't make love to her, right there, up against the coats hanging in the narrow hall.

And that wasn't likely to go down very well when he had been driving for five hours through the rush-hour traffic and the rain and the dark, was it? Lou took a steadying breath. No, let him come in, sit down, relax a bit. Then she could put her plan into action.

'Do you want a cup of tea?' she asked instead, backing away in case she brushed against him and ended up jumping him after all. 'Or something stronger?'

'Tea would be good,' said Patrick, rubbing a hand wearily over his face, and her heart clenched.

'Go and sit by the fire. I'll bring you a cup.'

Lou concentrated on breathing calmly as she waited for the kettle to boil. 'I can do this,' she told herself. 'I just need to be that match.'

When she carried the tea through into the sitting room Patrick was sitting on the sofa, his head dropped back and his eyes closed, but he stirred as she set the tray down on the stone hearth.

Lou had a moment's compunction. Maybe he was too tired for seduction? But tomorrow they were going back to London, and it would be so much harder once they were back in the usual routine with kids and homework and long days at the office.

She poured the tea and gave Patrick a mug, before sitting next to him with her own and gazing into the fire, taking courage from its merry blaze. Her relationship with Patrick could be that hot, if only she could find a way to convince him of that as well.

'How are the kids?' she asked. Pretty lame on the seduction front, but she had to start the conversation somewhere.

'They're fine,' he said. 'They'll be glad to have you back, though, and get back to normal.'

Lou sipped her tea. 'Funny, it's hard to remember what normal is now,' she said carefully. Perhaps this would be a good way to start the ball rolling?

'Our lives have changed so much this year,' she went on. 'It wasn't so long ago that normal was living in that cramped flat and taking the tube to work every morning. Since I've married you, there's been a whole new kind of normal. Not that you can really call our marriage normal, can you?'

'No, you can't.' It was too good an opening to miss, and Patrick decided to take the plunge. 'I guess most couples don't have the deal we do,' he said, equally cautious. 'And talking of that, Lou, there's something I think you should know.'

Lou went cold at the ominous phrase. He was going to tell her about some new girlfriend. Her cue was obvious. *What's that?* she was supposed to say, and then he would tell her about some long-legged blonde who had taken his fancy.

Unable to face hearing the words just yet, she rushed into speech. 'Actually, there's something you should know too,' she said. 'Something amazing, really.'

'Oh?' said Patrick, accepting his cue more readily than she had done.

'I went to see Fenny's solicitor yesterday,' Lou told him. 'Patrick, Fenny left me everything!'

'Surely you expected that?' he said gently.

'I knew she wanted to leave me the cottage, but I didn't think that there would be anything else,' said Lou. 'Fenny lived so frugally that I always assumed that she had to be careful with her pension. So much so that I can remember hoping that I would be able to afford to keep the cottage when the time came. I knew I would hate to sell it.'

She looked around the cosy sitting room, remembering the times she had sat there with her aunt. 'This is the closest I've got to a home.'

You've got a home with me, Patrick wanted to say, but didn't. Perhaps it didn't feel like home to Lou? The thought gave him a pang.

'Did she have some money put by, then?' he asked instead.

'A bit.' Lou's mouth twisted at the understatement, remembering how unprepared she had been when the solicitor had folded his hands and looked over his glasses at her.

'Your aunt was a very wealthy woman, Mrs Farr,' he said. 'I tried many times to get her to realise some of her assets to make her life more comfortable, but she always insisted that she had everything she wanted. She said that she couldn't be bothered to deal with it, and told me to invest it on your behalf. I naturally obeyed her instructions.'

The solicitor smiled a thin smile of restrained satisfaction. 'I have to tell you that you inherit a substantial amount of money, Mrs Farr.'

'I was flabbergasted,' Lou said, recounting the story to Patrick, who was listening with a sinking heart. 'I didn't have a clue that Fenny had any investments at all, and when he told me how much it was, I nearly passed out!'

Patrick put down his mug very carefully. 'It's a lot of money,' he said in a colourless voice.

'I know. He was full of advice about re-investing it, and thinking it through before I made any decisions. I think he thought that I was going to rush out and squander it all.'

'You should listen to him,' said Patrick. 'Think about what you really want and don't make any decisions in a hurry.'

'Well, I won't, but it's not as if anything's going to change, is it?' said Lou.

'Isn't it?' said Patrick flatly. 'I would have thought that everything was changed now.'

She stared at him. 'What do you mean?'

'You won't want to stay married to me any more, for a start,' he said with a forced smile. 'I know you miss Fenny badly, but if you'd known that this was going to happen, you wouldn't have made a deal like the one we made, would you?'

'No,' said Lou slowly.

She didn't like the way this conversation was going. She had only told him about the money to distract him from whatever he had been going to say, and now it looked as if she had given him another perfect opening. 'No, I wouldn't.'

'From what you've told me, you've got all the financial security you could ever want now,' said Patrick, trying to be fair, trying to be pleased for her, but all he could think was that she didn't need him any more.

Lou hadn't thought of it like that before. She hadn't really absorbed much beyond the fact that Fenny had been richer than she had ever imagined. Typical of her, really. She could have bought herself a new dress occasionally, or had a new range put in the kitchen, but Fenny had never bothered about things like that. As long as she could stay in the cottage and have her beloved garden, that was all she'd wanted.

'Yes, I suppose I have,' she said without enthusiasm.

Patrick took a deep breath. It wasn't fair on Lou to confuse the issue with emotions until she had absorbed all the implications of having financial independence of her own. She needed some time alone to think everything through.

'I'll quite understand if you want to reconsider the deal we made,' he said. 'I wouldn't contest a divorce.'

Lou couldn't believe that he was calmly sitting there, offering her a divorce, for all the world as if he didn't care one way or another. As if that was what he wanted.

Was that what he wanted?

She felt sick.

'What about you?' she said tightly. 'You wanted something from our deal too,' she reminded him.

Patrick avoided her eyes. 'Things have changed now. I don't want to make you stick to an agreement that doesn't make sense for you any more. We always agreed that we could divorce without any hard feelings.'

He might not have any hard feelings, but she certainly did. Lou was suddenly, gloriously, angry. If Patrick wanted out of their marriage, he could say so. She wasn't having him using her inheritance from Fenny as a convenient excuse to back out of an agreement that no longer suited him.

'Is reconsidering our deal what you wanted to talk about?' she asked him.

Patrick shifted uncomfortably. He didn't want to lie to her, but this obviously wasn't the time to tell her how he felt. 'Yes, in a way,' he said reluctantly.

'What's your problem with it?'

'I don't really want to talk about this now,' he said, cornered. Lou might not think that inheriting over two million pounds changed anything, but of course it did.

'Well, I do!' said Lou angrily. 'I think this is exactly the right time to talk about it. Tell me what you don't like about the deal we've got now.'

'It's too...constricting.'

'How? Have I ever made a fuss about you seeing anyone else?'

'No.'

'So you're just tired of the deal?'

'Yes,' Patrick admitted. At least he could be honest about that. 'I came here planning to ask you if you'd consider tearing up the pre-nuptial contract we both signed. And now that you're a wealthy woman in your own right, it's even more in your interests to think about doing just that.'

Lou had been gripping her mug of tea, but now she put it down on the tray and turned on the sofa so that one leg was tucked up beneath her.

'I want you to be honest with me,' she said, keeping her voice steady with an effort. 'Have you met someone else?'

'No.'

'So you don't want to marry anyone else?'

'God, no,' said Patrick, appalled.

'OK.' Lou tried to think of another reason why he might want to end the marriage, as it sounded as if he did. 'Do you just not want to be married?'

'No!' he protested, goaded into the truth at last. 'I like being married. I like being married to *you*,' he amended. 'I like coming home and finding you there. I like Grace and Tom. I like the way the house feels like a home. I like the mess and the noise and the fact that you've unpicked everything I paid that garden designer a fortune to do. I'm used to you,' he told her. 'I miss you when you're not there,' he said almost accusingly.

Lou's anger began to evaporate. She could feel it fizzling out of her as a tiny glimmer of hope uncurled deep inside. 'So what's wrong?'

'The deal's wrong.' Patrick ran a hand despairingly through his hair. 'I hate it that I can't touch you. I hate that when I come in you don't kiss me. I hate having separate rooms. Of *course* there isn't anyone else! I don't *want* anyone else. I just want you,' he finished, sounding defeated.

'I love you,' he said simply as Lou sat there, stunned. 'I

thought about you all the way up the motorway tonight. I planned what I was going to say. I was going to tell you how I felt and ask you if you would forget that stupid deal, if we could be married like normal people, arguing sometimes, and getting in a muddle but talking about it and getting through it, and loving each other… And now you tell me don't need me any more.'

Surprise helped Lou find her tongue. 'When did I say that?'

'Just now. Fenny's bequest has left you financially independent.'

'That's true,' she said, marvelling that he could be so dense. 'I don't need your money,' she agreed. 'But I need other things, Patrick. I need you to make me tea when I'm tired. I need you to help me deal with the kids. I need you to drive me up and down the country and be there for me the way you've been there for the last few weeks.

'But most of all, I need to see you. I need to know that you'll come home to me. I need to be able to reach out and touch you whenever I want.'

A smile hovered around her mouth. 'And what I need absolutely most of all is for you to kiss me.'

Patrick was staring at her, as if unable to believe what he was hearing.

'Now,' she prompted in case he had misunderstood, and a smile that started deep in his eyes spread over his face.

'If you insist,' he said, and Lou leant to meet him halfway, and then they were kissing, deep, sweet kisses that went on and on as they shifted to get closer, wriggling to touch, to press against each other, to feel each other. Patrick's hands were sliding under her jumper, hot against her skin, exploring her, unlocking her until she sighed with pleasure.

'I need you to love me,' she whispered between kisses. 'Do you think you can do that?'

Patrick pulled her down so that she slid underneath him. 'Yes, I can do that,' he said, kissing her throat, his lips warm and possessive, and she shivered luxuriously.

'Only me? Nobody else?'

He paused and lifted his head. 'What, not Grace and Tom?'

'No, I don't mind you loving them,' she conceded, pulling his shirt free of his trousers.

'What about my mother?' he teased her.

'Nobody young and beautiful that you're not related to,' said Lou, trying to sound stern, but it was hard when his hand was curved over her breast and his smile was warm against her skin.

'No, I won't love anyone like that,' he promised. 'I'll just love you...and my car. You don't mind that, do you?'

Lou smiled and wound her arms around his neck. 'I can live with that,' she said and sank back into his kisses.

'You're the only woman I've ever loved like this,' Patrick told her shakily a little later. 'You're the only one I've ever wanted like this. I haven't been able to think about another woman since that night in Newcastle.'

'Ha, and I suppose you were just playing tiddly-winks with Ariel in the Maldives!'

His lips twitched. 'I only took her to prove to myself that I wasn't obsessed with you, and it didn't work.'

'I don't believe you were obsessed with me at all!'

'I was. Utterly. I have been ever since I looked over that table and wondered whether you were wearing stockings or not. After that I couldn't *stop* wondering. I used to fantasise about you all the time.' He looked down into Lou's dark eyes. 'You can tell me now. Were you wearing stockings under all those little suits?'

Lou smiled and put his hand on her knee. 'Why don't you find out?' she whispered.

Patrick's hand slid under her skirt, feeling the warmth of her thigh beneath its sheer covering, drifting upwards until he caught his breath as his fingers found the top of the stocking, the clip on the suspender belt.

'If we weren't already married, I would ask you to marry me,' he said, his voice ragged with desire.

'And I'd say yes,' said Lou, no steadier.

'Would you? Would you marry me, not my money?'

'If you'd promise to love me for ever and not even look at a blonde again.'

'I promise,' he said seriously.

'It looks as if we won't be needing that divorce after all, then,' she said. 'You're stuck with me.'

Patrick laughed and pulled her closer. 'You're the only one I want to be stuck with!' he said as he kissed her again.

'You know, I had a plan to seduce you this evening,' said Lou breathlessly, long delicious minutes later. She wriggled on top of him so that her hair swung down and tickled his face and began to unbutton his shirt, kissing his chest as she went.

'That's the trouble with you middle-aged women,' Patrick pretended to grumble. 'You're only interested in sex. You haven't even told me that you love me!'

Lou kissed her way back up his throat. 'I love you,' she said, dropping soft kisses on his mouth between each promise. 'I love you, I love you, I love you.'

Patrick smiled against her kisses. 'It looks like you're going to get lucky, then,' he said, and rolled her over so that they slid off the sofa onto the hearthrug. His hands were warm on her thigh, fingering the top of her stocking, and Lou forgot about the need for a match. Their very own fire was already blazing high, and nothing could stop it now.

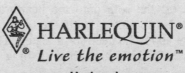

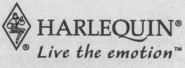

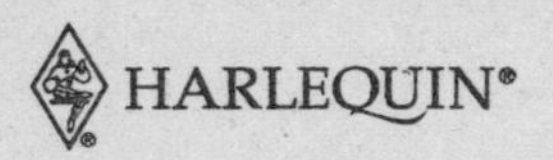

HARLEQUIN ROMANCE®

Coming Next Month

#3863 MARRIAGE AT MURRAREE Margaret Way

Discovering her father was a billionaire cattle king makes Casey McGuire one of the famous "McIvor heiresses." She's worked hard all her life, but she's never had the prospect of money—until now. Nor has she ever truly known love, but irresistible Troy Connellan is ready to change all that. Can wary Casey let go of her past for a future with a rich, powerful—gorgeous—man?

The McIvor Sisters

#3864 WINNING BACK HIS WIFE Barbara McMahon

Heather's ex-husband is back! Hunter never understood why Heather walked out. Even when she confesses the truth, it seems too much has happened for a reconciliation. But Heather can see the attraction is still there—and, deep down, so is the love....

#3865 JUST FRIENDS TO...JUST MARRIED Renee Roszel

Kimberly Albert's boyfriend has just walked out and she needs the one man who's always been there for her: her best friend, Jaxon Gideon. But Jax can't be Kim's shoulder to cry on—he's in love with her. So he decides that if he can't have Kim in his life, he wants her out of it! But Kim's starting to see a new side to Jax—an irresistible, sexy side—and she likes what she sees!

#3866 IMPOSSIBLY PREGNANT Nicola Marsh

Keely Rhodes can't believe her luck when gorgeous Lachlan Brant hires her to design a new Web site for his radio show. The girls at the office think Lachlan is Keely's perfect man, and they tell her to go for it! But after Keely's business/pleasure trip away, she's got more gossip—what she'd thought impossible has happened: she's pregnant with Lachlan's baby!

Office Gossip

HRCNM0905